His a[illegible]
was i[illegible]

"You look as though you want to eat me up," Tess said, her words wrapped in a sigh.

Cord brushed aside love-tossed strands of hair from her breasts so that his gaze could roam unhindered. "You read my mind."

She flushed at his suggestive tone, and he grinned. "We have to pass the time some way. I'm no superman." He rolled off her, and she relished the quiver of heightened sensation that even their parting caused.

She let her fingers drift over his lean nakedness. He reminded her of a sleek panther, and she felt new fire burst to life in her core. It surprised her and she smiled, delighted with the Tessa Jane that Cord's lovemaking had created.

"You don't give yourself enough credit," she murmured, her gaze following the downward trail of her hand. "In fact, right now you feel a lot like the man of steel to me."

Renee Roszel feels that one of the best things about writing romances is having the opportunity to meet dynamic, interesting people while developing story ideas. After reading an article about the mythical Champ—Lake Champlain's answer to the Loch Ness monster—Renee tracked down one of the nation's foremost Champ researchers, Joseph W. Zarzynski. She says that his personal charm coupled with Champ's aloof appeal made *Legendary Lover* her favorite effort to date, and she wishes her two new friends—Zarr and Champ—a lofty place in scientific history.

Books by Renee Roszel

HARLEQUIN TEMPTATION

246–ANOTHER HEAVEN

Legendary Lover

RENEE ROSZEL

Harlequin Books

TORONTO • NEW YORK • LONDON
AMSTERDAM • PARIS • SYDNEY • HAMBURG
STOCKHOLM • ATHENS • TOKYO • MILAN

To Stacie Cabral
and Malinda Harris
for finding me
when I needed finding

Published December 1989

ISBN 0-373-25379-6

Printed in U.S.A.

Prologue

FROM HER CROUCHED POSITION in the underbrush behind the pole barn, Tessa Jane had no trouble spotting Cord. He was the most magnificent sight any red-blooded sixteen-year-old girl could hope to see. She'd only been at Broken Arrow High School since Christmas, when her father had landed the gas station job, but she felt as if she'd been in love with Cord Redigo all her life.

With that wavy blond hair, those clear blue eyes and that muscular body, he was the most gorgeous hunk who'd ever walked the face of the earth. And that smile... When he grinned, there was a devil-may-care lift to one corner that turned her to mush. She wished, just once, he'd aim that smile her way.

Last week Tessa Jane's father had been fired for being drunk on the job. It had become a familiar story since her mother's death four years ago. At least, this time, her dad's boss allowed them to stay in the gas station's tiny apartment until Tessa Jane finished the final week of her sophomore year. That time was up today. First thing tomorrow they'd be hitching rides along the highway—broke and homeless, again. Tessa

Jane Mankiller would be gone, and Cord Redigo would never even know she existed.

The sun had become an orange disk in the west. Eight flat-bed hay wagons were overflowing with carefree, graduating seniors. Tessa Jane's throat closed as she heard the stirring timbre of Cord's laughter. The silver belt buckle he wore flashed golden in the setting sun as he helped his pretty blond girlfriend onto the end wagon.

On legs aching badly from her long, cramped wait, she edged up to a junker pickup, her heart fluttering like a barnful of frightened chickens. She absolutely had to talk to him—just once—before she left town.

When the sun dropped below the horizon, the tractor engines rumbled to life, signaling Tessa Jane's last chance to meet Cord—to be the recipient of his brilliant smile. She scurried across the gaping space and scrambled onto the end hay wagon. Without daring to breathe, she secreted herself behind a stack of quilts.

She peered over them, her eyes fastening on the vague outline of Cord's rugged profile. When he bent to kiss Marissa, Tessa Jane turned away.

Time dragged as the tractors slowly pulled the wagons along the dirt roads that criss-crossed the Redigo property. After an hour, they reached a huge bonfire, circled the wagons and the teens clambered down to gather around the fire.

When everybody had gone, Tessa Jane sat up and peered around. They were deep into the Redigo property, miles from the main road. It was dark—very dark. She didn't know which would be more stupid at this point, trying to find her way back, or staying on the hay wagon like the pesky snoop she was.

Just as she was about to opt for getting out of there, no matter what the consequences, she was halted by an unexpected turn of events.

"Okay, Mr. Valedictorian!" one of the girls shouted. "If you're so smart, you be first under the blanket for 'Guess the Girl.'"

The crowd around them rumbled with laughter as another girl chimed in, "Come on, Cord. I bet you can't guess me."

"You chicken?" taunted a husky young man that Tessa Jane recognized to be the captain of the football team.

Cord exhaled, shaking his head. "Rob, this is dumb. . . ."

"I'll go first," Marissa announced a little belligerently.

Rob slung an arm around her neck. "Oh, no, you don't. Girlfriends are ineligible for obvious reasons."

"By whose rules?" she shot back.

He ignored her. "Cord, get up there under that blanket. I'll choose who goes first." With a harassing pinch on Cord's cheek, he added, "Show us a little guts."

The cluster of people was growing, and so were the catcalls and needling shouts. Cord gave up with a shrug, and hoisted himself onto the wagon. Tessa Jane shrank back into the deep nest of hay and lay very still.

When Cord drew the blanket over his head, Tessa Jane heard Marissa whisper to Rob, "Didn't you say you brought some booze?"

"Yeah, you thirsty?" He pulled a flask from his back pocket.

"Very!" She snatched the bottle, and when the first pretty candidate had been lifted up to join Cord, Marissa grabbed a quilt and stalked around the wagon to plop down in the darkness.

Tessa Jane stared wide-eyed as the game progressed. Marissa had gulped down most of the contents of the flask, calling Rob a nag when he tried to take it away from her as the sixth girl took her turn at trying to fool Cord. The newcomer failed.

After the seventh girl crawled out, Rob called it quits. "Cord, this is getting boring. Besides, Marissa's mad." When Cord started to crawl out, Rob pushed his head back under. "Stay there. You've earned some time alone with your girl. Come on the rest of you, Hank and Teddy are tuning up for the sing-along."

As the others straggled away, Cord called Marissa's name.

Tessa Jane knew she had to leave now. The last thing she wanted to witness was Cord and Marissa moaning and writhing beneath a blanket. She was just about to scramble over the side when she heard a faint groan, and saw Marissa's head disappear below the wagon.

Crawling to the edge, she looked down. The pretty blonde had passed out cold on her blanket.

"Marissa," Cord repeated. "Are you coming?"

Tessa Jane wavered. She could make a clean getaway, or she could tell Cord that his girl wasn't coming. She stared at the blanket, her insides aching. She hesitated for only an instant before crawling over to him, planning to tell him about Marissa.

Before she could say anything, a large hand grasped her wrist and pulled her beneath the blanket. She sucked in a surprised gasp. When she tried to tell him he'd made a terrible mistake, she discovered that her ability to form words was gone.

He'd wrapped his arms around her, but his movement stopped abruptly on the rounded curve of Tessa Jane's hip. "Who are you?" he asked. "You're not Marissa."

"No . . . ," she managed in a reedy whisper.

He chuckled. "I thought the game was over."

She could feel the warmth of his breath on her face and she smiled, despite her nervousness. "It is." Her voice sounded husky in her ears, and she swallowed several times to ease the dryness in her throat. "Marissa, er, passed out."

"Damn. Is she okay?"

"She's asleep on a blanket—everybody else has gone off to sing, Cord. I just wanted—"

"You wanted to see if I could guess who you are," he finished for her, sounding a little tired. "Okay." He moved his hands to her shoulders. "Marissa's better off asleep than sick, I guess."

He moved his face so close to hers, she could feel his curls graze her cheek. "What are you doing?" she asked, her voice more high-pitched than she'd intended.

"Sniffing. You aren't wearing perfume."

"No." She blanched, embarrassed. Perfume was a luxury she couldn't afford.

"You're an Ivory girl," he whispered. "That's refreshing."

A shiver ran down her spine as his lips accidentally brushed her chin. "Thank you," she murmured inanely.

His hands had moved up to cup her ears. He touched the lobes. "No earrings? No fair. They're a dead giveaway."

"Well—I—"

"I know. You didn't want to make it too easy for me."

She chewed on the inside of her cheek. How horribly beneath him in class she was—entirely too poor.

He ran his fingers through her short hair. "Soft," he murmured. "A no-nonsense woman. I like that."

Her cheeks grew hot. A no-nonsense woman. She'd never thought of herself that way. If she was, it was out of necessity, but she enjoyed the idea that Cord liked her that way.

"May I touch your face?" he asked quietly.

"Why. . . sure."

He ran his thumbs over her closed eyelids. "Lord, you have thick eyelashes. I bet they're black."

His unexpected remark startled her. "Why?"

"A guess. Blondes don't have thick lashes, usually."

"You're very observant of women, aren't you?"

"I try to be observant of everything. Don't you?"

He had her there. "I—guess."

"If you're not blond, that cuts about twenty percent of the girls I know. Your lips?"

"I have two. Does that cut out any girls you know?"

He laughed. "You have a sense of humor. That shuts out about fifty percent. No. I meant, may I touch your lips?"

"Be my guest." Though she didn't say so, she would have given up breathing to have him touch her lips.

His fingers slowly traced her mouth. She greedily inhaled the aroma of his hand, a pleasant mixture of smoke from the wood fire and his own musky maleness. His scent mingled nicely with the dusty-sweet smell of the hay, and she felt strangely at home. His hard, male torso beckoned, and Tessa Jane began to experience an unfamiliar urgency in the pit of her stomach.

"You have very full lips," he was remarking, as though he was concentrating on their shape, trying to picture them. "I bet you have a nice smile."

"You have a nice smile," she blurted, unable to help herself.

"Thanks." He sounded a little surprised. Touching her chin he remarked, "I give up, mystery lady. You've stumped me. Let's get out from under here so I can see who—"

As he moved to lift the blanket off of them, she grasped his wrist. "No, Cord. Wait." Her body was pricked through with needles of fear, but she knew if she backed out now, she'd regret it for the rest of her life. "Cord . . . ?" She touched his chest with both her palms. "Would you . . . kiss me?"

There was a long pause before he probed softly, "Why? You lose a bet?"

"You're teasing me," she mumbled miserably.

"Maybe a little," he offered gently. "But if it's a kiss you want . . ."

He bent his face to hers, finding her mouth. Tessa Jane's knowledge in the matter of kissing was badly limited. She was thankful she didn't crash into his teeth. Though brief, his kiss was the most significant sensation Tessa Jane could ever remember. His lips had been firm, but yielding, and he'd tasted so good.

"Who are you . . . ?" he asked, his voice a tinge huskier than before.

With a strength born of desperation, she pulled his face to hers. Running on pure instinct now, she wriggled closer until her body was tight against his. He groaned against her lips.

She lifted her face, her tongue darting out, teasing the corner of his mouth. An instant later, he was kissing her. This time there was nothing tentative or brief about the act. His arms moved around to pull her even more intimately to him. He opened his lips.

Learning quickly now, Tessa Jane followed suit. When their tongues met, she sighed, and her whole body softened against his, molding to his hard, lean frame.

His hands began to explore. When he cupped her hips, she groaned. He pulled his lips a hair's breadth away. "What in hell are we—"

"I love you, Cord," she cried softly. She knew in the depths of her soul that this was right. She felt that so strongly that nothing, short of Cord bolting from the wagon, could stop what they had set in motion.

He mumbled something that sounded vaguely biblical. She didn't know if it was a curse or a prayer, and she didn't care. The young man she loved was holding her in his arms, kissing her with hot, demanding lips. While a slightly off-key rendition of a Johnny Cash ballad rang out amid laughter and talking, Tessa Jane was relieved of her panties.

Cord's fingers began to explore her most private, secret self, and she hugged him to her, shedding tears of happiness. She gasped at delightful, newborn sensations deep inside her, as he took her lips with his.

Lifting shaky fingers, she stroked his hair. It felt like strands of silk between her fingers.

"Oh, Cord!" she half-cried, half-whimpered as her body exploded with red-hot delight. She pulled him to her, holding his wonderful solidness against her pounding heart as passion's sweet nectar seeped through her like a warm, addictive narcotic.

He was holding her tenderly, not speaking. Her naked thighs were entangled with his legs. After a moment or two, the ultimate sensation had begun to subside, and she realized that Cord had given her a gift and received nothing in return. Kissing his jaw, she took his belt buckle between her trembling fingers and helped him pull his jeans down.

He surprised her by taking her hand and closing her fingers around him. At first the intimacy frightened her. She had not anticipated his size, and she had sudden, tremendous doubts that this thing that was happening between them could possibly work. But he took her hand, whispering, "Guide me." Somehow the soft assurance in his voice calmed her fears. She knew she could not only do this for him, but it would be perfect for them both.

They were lying side by side. He took her hips in his hands and pressed her toward him as she did as he'd told her. It surprised her to realize how damp she had become.

As she pressed him into her, Cord groaned. Kissing her forehead, he moved his hips to unite them more deeply. It surprised him when he met resistance. "What the hell?" He drew away slightly. "You're a vir—"

"No!" She pressed herself hard against him, cringing at the rending pain her impetuous thrust had cost her. She clung to him, kissing his cheek, his jaw, his lips, murmuring, "It's okay... really...."

When Cord's shock had waned slightly, he was being kissed and reassured so sweetly that his raging hormones allowed him little choice but to respond in kind. He returned her kisses, and they grew deeper, his tongue finding hers in a teasing, taunting dance that made him burn with need. He began to move against her, tentatively at first, making sure that he wasn't hurting her. Even though he hated the fact that he'd just taken a total stranger's virginity, the crazy situation had gone too far. Not even a saint could back away now, especially a nineteen-year-old one.

Tessa Jane shuddered and whimpered his name, grasping him to her as her body quaked with spasms of pleasure. "Oh—oh—Cord. I've never felt this way...."

He could feel her tears against his cheek as he found his own release. He clung to her, too, feeling a strange protectiveness for this petite young woman with the scent of soap, and the soft, sexy mouth. She was so beautifully naive in his arms. It wasn't as though he'd made love to all that many young women, but the ones he had slept with had been experienced partners. He relished the sweetness of the moment with his unknown, virginal lover for as long as he dared.

There were over 160 of his friends not fifty feet away, not to mention his steady girlfriend, passed out somewhere beneath them. At least he hoped she was still unaware of where he was and what he was doing.

But this girl—whoever she was—had taken him so by surprise, with her timid kisses and whispers of love.... Well, *hell*, he'd done it now. He'd regret it tomorrow, but now...

When his heartbeat had returned to a relatively normal rate, he murmured, "Don't you think it's about time I knew your name?"

"Tessa Jane." The words came out on a sweet, languid sigh.

"Tessa Jane what?"

She smiled dreamily, hoping that very soon her last name would be Redigo. "Does it matter?"

He didn't know what possessed him, but he couldn't resist kissing the tip of her nose. "You're a very strange young woman, Tessa Jane." Patting her hip, he told her huskily, "We'd better get presentable. I don't think the Waco brothers have that large a reserve of songs."

When he'd adjusted his clothes, he lifted the blanket and looked down at her. His smile faded, and he stared.

"What's the matter?" she asked, feeling a rush of panic.

"Hell . . ." He frowned. "You're just a kid. How old are you, anyway? Fourteen?"

"I turned sixteen two months ago." She sat up, running a hand through her tangled hair. Straw fell around her.

"Oh, that's great, Redigo." He shook his head. "Children, yet!"

His disgusted remark was like a slap. All of a sudden Tessa Jane saw the stark reality of what she'd done—what she'd lost. And what was worse, Cord thought she was a child! She shrank back in the hay, mortified.

The rest of the hayride went by in a blur for Tessa Jane. Marissa felt so awful that she accepted Cord's explanation that he was giving one of the "hands' kids" a ride home. After he'd let Marissa out at her rambling ranch-style house, he climbed back into his car and turned unhappy eyes on her. "Okay. Where do you live, Tessa Jane?"

She felt tacky and out of place in the plush red leather bucket seat. She hurt between her legs, and she hurt in her heart. She dropped her gaze to her lap and didn't answer.

"Did you hear me?"

"Yes," she muttered. "And the name's Mankiller. Tessa Jane Mankiller."

"Mankiller," he repeated, his tone brimming with frustration. She could see his fists tighten around the steering wheel. "What were you doing tonight? Trying to live up to it?"

She pestered her lower lip with her teeth, changing the subject. "I live in an apartment over Potter's Discount Gas."

"Are you all right?" He seemed sincere. She guessed she should appreciate his concern, however begrudgingly it might be given.

She sighed but didn't say anything.

He turned out of the quiet suburb and headed toward downtown. "That wasn't very bright, you know—what you did." With a vehemence that made Tessa Jane jump, he pounded a fist on his burled wood dashboard. "Damn! Who am I to talk? That was the most lame-brained thing I've ever done!"

She slanted a gaze at him through her lashes. What had been the singularly most important event of her life had been the most lame-brained act of his. She bit back a sob.

His scowling profile was indistinct through her hovering tears. "I thought I...I loved you." Her whisper was laced with heated emotion. "I *don't*."

He exhaled long and low. "You're a kid. You don't know anything about love. Hell. I don't know that much about it myself."

Tessa Jane wiped at a tear and turned to stare, unseeing, out the window. The world slid by at a rapid clip. Cord was certainly in a hurry to be rid of her.

They rode the rest of the way in silence. The station was closed and dark. One dingy streetlight illuminated the corner where Cord pulled in. He surprised her by getting out and walking around to her door to assist her. He took her hand, but she yanked it away, pushing past him. "Don't bother."

"Dammit!" He took her by the shoulders and turned her to face him. "Promise me you won't do anything so foolish again."

She lifted her chin. Clinging to the remnants of her tattered pride, she assured him, "Don't worry about me. I'll be fine." Feeling bitterly rejected, Tessa Jane brushed his hands from her shoulders, mumbling harshly, "Please—go away."

Wanting to comfort her in some small way, he reached toward her, but saw the warning in her eyes. Defeated, he shrugged his hands into his pockets. "Look, Tessa Jane. I'm sorry about what happened tonight. . . ."

She said nothing. She just continued to stare at him. In the dreadful silence, a tear slid down her face. For the first time in his life, Cord was at a complete loss. He felt like a rat deserting a sinking ship, but there was little else he could do now. In a subdued voice, he whispered, "Goodbye, Tessa Jane."

Dragging his eyes from her distraught face, he walked around his car and slid behind the wheel. As he drove out of the station, he could see her in his rearview mirror. She stood stiffly, her slim body washed in harsh, yellow light while she endured his retreat with a gritty, admirable pride. He ground out a blasphemy, knowing he'd never be able to forget the pain in her glistening, green eyes.

1

Thirteen years later. . .

TESS WAS RUNNING LATE. Eight new guests were arriving at four o'clock, and naturally, room twelve's plumbing had gone on the blink. Hurrying down the Georgian staircase, she dashed through the cozy reception hall to the front desk. Kalvin was sound asleep, snoring, his straggly blond head resting on his forearms.

She heaved a distracted sigh. "Any messages, Kal?" she asked, her voice pitched loud enough to snap him awake.

He bobbed up, rubbing his eyes with bony fists. Blinking, he tried to focus on whoever it was who'd awakened him.

Tess glanced at her watch. It was nearly noon. "Good morning, Kalvin," she teased. "Up late last night?"

He responded with a gap-toothed grin. "Oh hullo, Ms Mankiller." He scraped a big paw through his sandy hair and yawned. "Yep. Out watchin' the water."

"See anything of Champ?" She was interested, but not very hopeful. Lake Champlain's monster was legendary, but his presence was yet undocumented.

She'd lived in Lost Cove Inn, near Vergennes, Vermont, for nearly twelve years, and hadn't seen Champ herself. Still, there were enough reported sightings every year to keep her hoping. The legend of Champ was what brought most of their guests to the inn. Therefore, she chose to believe in him.

"Nah." Kalvin flipped a hand in the air. "Thought I did a couple of times, but the fog was pretty thick. Couldn't prove nothin'."

"Well," she said, smiling at him. "Don't fret about it. If Champ's out there, you'll see him."

"Heck, Ms Mankiller, I've seen him a bunch of times. Just never had no witnesses."

"You need to keep your camera with you," she suggested, reaching for the telephone notepad.

"Easy to say," he groused. "Seems like ol' Champ always shows his self when I'm weedin' or dumpin' trash. He stays good and hid when I'm ready for him."

Tess laughed, thumbing through the messages. "You know what they say—'a watched pot never boils.'"

"Huh?"

"Never mind." Her attention was riveted on a message. Kalvin's handwriting was not easy to read, so she was sure she was mistaken about the name, but her stomach lurched. It irritated her to think that even a scrawled name that resembled Redigo could affect her so strongly after all these years. Shoving the pad under Kalvin's nose, she asked, "What does this say?"

He squinted down at it. "Uh, says that group from the university's made a change in their reservations."

"What about the reservations?"

Kalvin scratched his ear. "Well, near as I could make out, the other woman zoo teacher—"

"Zoology professor," Tess interrupted gently.

"Uh, I guess. Anyway, the other lady who was comin' with Ms Cash can't make it, so a guy's comin' in her place. Since Ms Cash and the other lady doc was sharin' a room, this guy called to say he'd need a room of his own."

"This guy?" Tess repeated.

"Yeah—name was Red somethin'."

"Redigo?" She dragged a strand of her waist-length hair across her shoulder and began to fiddle with it.

"Yeah, somethin' like that."

"Did he leave his first name?"

"Nope, can't say he did. He was a doc, though."

"Well, never mind." She swept her hair back, trying to shake off her sudden unease. "Say, Kalvin. Do you have a cigarette?"

He squinted at her. "No, ma'am. You know I don't smoke them things."

"Oh, right." She fumbled in her slacks pocket for change. "Listen, room twelve's stopped up again. We're going to need it by four, when they arrive."

"No chance."

Tess had started around the desk, heading for the cigarette machine, when his words stopped her. "What do you mean?"

"Already checked it out. Needs a part. Barney's Plumbing's gettin' right on orderin' it for me."

"Ordering it?" She grimaced. "Well, how long...?"

"Don't know. Maybe a week."

"Fine . . ." She sighed, fighting frustration. "Okay, when they get here, put Dr. Red-whatever in the overflow room."

"Yes ma'am. Ms Mankiller?"

"What?" She drummed her fingers on the polished oak, unaccountably nervous.

"I thought you said you was gonna quit smokin'."

"I am. I'm going to." She headed toward the cigarettes. "Just not today."

"Oh," Kalvin murmured, sounding befuddled. "That's good, I guess."

It can't possibly be Cord Redigo, she told herself as she dropped the coins into the machine. Just last November she'd seen that article in the *Smithsonian* magazine about him. According to the article, he was doing research in the Indian Ocean and living on some island near Madagascar—the other side of the world. It was ridiculous to think that this male doctor Red-whatever could possibly be her "Big-Mistake-in-the-Hay-Redigo."

She lit a cigarette and took a puff, inhaling deeply. Besides, the way Kalvin took phone messages, the doctor's name could be anything from Redbird to Redtape. She took another drag on the cigarette, feeling better. It had just been her need for nicotine that had made her so antsy, she rationalized. She was fine now.

Crushing out the cigarette with yet another vow that this was absolutely her very last one, she headed down the back hall. The inn wouldn't run itself.

TESS CHECKED her watch again. Five-thirty. Dr. Cash's party was late. That didn't bother her. Guests arrived late all the time. The thing that had been wearing on her nerves was the fact that she hadn't been able to put Cord Redigo from her thoughts. Boy, had she been young and naive when she'd crawled under that blanket. She wished it had never happened, but since it had, she'd spent a lot of years working awfully hard to put it completely behind her.

Her past was another world, another life. All she wanted was to be able to stuff that night into some little corner of her brain and forget it. Until this Red-something person arrived to ease her mind that it really wasn't Cord Redigo, she was going to have the gnawing feeling that a shotgun was aimed at her chest, cocked and ready to fire.

Her nerves in tatters, she dropped her aunt's dinner tray on the kitchen countertop with a clatter. Turning to reassure her cook, Sugar Smith, that nothing had broken, she realized she needn't have bothered. Sugar had on earphones connected to a tiny recorder fastened to her belt. Totally oblivious, she was gyrating her ample hips back and forth as she stood in front of the cutting board slicing carrots.

Tess tapped her on the shoulder. She knew from experience that when Sugar was absorbed in one of her blaring Elvis, Beach Boys or Cher tapes, any attempt at conversation would be futile.

Sugar turned around and grinned, her plump, middle-age face flushed from the kitchen's heat. With a wet hand, she gingerly moved one of the earphones forward to rest on her cheek. "Hi, boss. What can I do for you . . . ?"

"Just checking about dinner," Tess half-shouted. "Looks like the weather's going to hold. Let's serve on the terrace in the garden. It'll be a nice change. Virge'll need to get the extra tables set up."

Sugar nodded, answering in a singsong voice, "Check. I'll wake my sweetie pie."

"Is that a lyric or is Virge napping?"

Sugar laughed. "Just taking a little break." She wagged her heavy shoulders to the beat as she replaced the earphone. "Tables'll be set up, no prob, boss—baby—baby—"

Tess had another thought, but decided against attempting to break through the noise barrier. Sugar was already heading toward the kitchen's back door, lost in her rock-and-roll paradise.

"Boss, baby—catchy. Maybe I ought to put it on my office door." She smiled at the absurd idea.

"I know *I'd* knock," a deep voice remarked as she turned to go.

She stumbled to a halt when she saw the lanky, blond man in the doorway. He was carrying two suitcases. A slow, slightly crooked smile sauntered across his lips. It took all her strength to keep from gaping in horror. Cord Redigo had stepped quietly back into her life. The shotgun that had been aimed at her chest all afternoon finally exploded, ripping a hole through her.

She stood there, frozen, and all he could do was grin at her and look like the American cowboy incarnate. He exuded wealth, though he was casually dressed in a herringbone Harris tweed western jacket, denim shirt and brushed cotton pants. And he was absolutely gorgeous, damn him! The same charismatic man she remembered, only with the added allure of maturity. His skin was darkly tanned. His blond hair was longer than she remembered. Sun-streaked to a glossy platinum, it fell in waves to kiss the collar of his jacket.

She realized with some irritation that she was unable to pull her gaze away from the twinkle in his eyes. She remembered that twinkle and felt a surge of pain. Her paralysis was stupid, and she hated herself for falling prey to Cord's physical beauty again.

"Hi, boss baby," he said, still grinning. "Someone named Kalvin told me I could get to my room by way of the kitchen stairs." He lifted an apologetic shoulder. "Apparently I've caused some trouble by being a man."

She had a nasty urge to tell him exactly how true that statement was. She had no idea how many other women he'd caused trouble for just by being a man, but seeing him standing there in all his raging masculinity, she could only guess that they were legion.

With great difficulty she managed to put on her innkeeper's smile. "Not really, it's just that we're having a little plumbing problem in the room you were to have occupied. I think you'll find this other room quite adequate, if you don't mind being separated from your friends."

"No problem. They're all strangers, except my cousin Mary, and there are moments when she doesn't love me all that much."

His grin was bold, teasing. She urged herself to ignore it. "Let me get one of these bags for you."

"I can handle them."

"But your room's on the third floor."

"Thanks for the warning, but I can manage."

She tried to pretend nonchalance, but she was irked by the amused glint in his eyes. She knew he was laughing at her, thinking that just because she was only five foot four, she couldn't carry a measly suitcase up three flights of stairs. At least, he hadn't recognized her. That was a blessing, anyway. "Well, then, if you'll follow me. . . ."

"Oh, Ms—" Kalvin crashed through the swinging door into Cord's back. "Oops! Sorry, Doc." He stepped disjointedly aside and addressed Tess. "Uh, I was wonderin' if you want me to unpack them cases of soap that come in today?"

"What about the front desk?" Tess asked.

"Penny's back. Says the doctor told her she's got a allergy—it ain't flu."

"Oh, well, good." Tess nodded. "Thanks for helping out, Kalvin. Go on and unpack the soap, then have your dinner."

Kalvin smiled at her and turned to Cord. "Ya want me to help you with them bags, Doc?"

"No, thanks. And call me Cord."

"That's mighty nice." Kalvin beamed, appreciating the doctor's thoughtfulness.

"And you." Cord turned back to face Tess. "Do you have a name besides boss baby?"

"My name?" With the weak repetition of his question, Cord's expression grew slightly quizzical. He seemed to be wondering if her name had slipped her mind. Or perhaps he was trying to recall where he'd seen her before.

She had little time to think, she only knew that he couldn't help but remember her if he heard the name Mankiller. It was fruitless to believe he could stay at the inn for the whole month of June and never hear her last name, but just now she wasn't prepared for the look of recognition in his eyes, be it shock, or worse, pity.

Taking the cowardly way out, she said, "Tess—call me Tess, we're all one big family here, right, Kalvin?"

"Huh?" he asked, staring at her as though she'd just eaten a frog.

"Never mind." She sighed, wanting to get out of this as quickly as possible. "You get busy with that soap." Motioning toward the far corner of the kitchen where the stairs were located, she said, "Dr. Redigo, please follow me."

"How did you know my name was Redigo?"

She grimaced. Luckily, he was behind her and couldn't see her face. She mumbled, "I check phone messages."

When they'd reached his door, Tess was desperate to get away. She hadn't felt this shaken in years. She had no idea what had happened to her knees back on the last landing, but she'd stumbled right in front of him. No doubt he'd dub her a total klutz. She hadn't dared look at him, but she knew what he must have been thinking. How could she have carried one of his bags if she couldn't even walk adequately? It was probably a very good point. She didn't plan to debate it, she just planned to get quickly away.

"Thanks again, Tess." He put his suitcases down and extended his hand.

She looked at his hand with the same enthusiasm she would have shown a ticking bomb. His fingers were long, tanned a golden brown, with immaculately trimmed nails. She noticed that he wore no rings. She hesitated. Refusing to shake his hand would be very rude, and after a pause that she hoped hadn't been too obvious, she accepted it.

His fingers were warm, firm and surprisingly callused. He may be a rich man, she thought, but he didn't shrink from physical labor. The word *physical* raked at her memory and her cheeks grew hot. She was grateful she wasn't inclined to blush. "You're welcome, Dr. Redigo. I hope you enjoy your room."

"Call me Cord," he corrected. "I thought we were all one big happy family around here."

His steady gaze held hers. Though his smile was friendly, it had an unnerving quality that continued to fluster her. Forcing herself to think of business, she said, "Maybe I'd better warn you, you'll be sharing a bath. I hope that isn't too much of an inconvenience."

"Sounds a little kinky," he remarked with an unabashed grin.

She blinked. "No—I meant the *room*."

"Oh. My mistake." His blue eyes sparkled with fun at her expense. "No problem. I've shared a bathroom before."

I'll just bet, she scoffed inwardly. Determined to remain polite, she asked, "Do you usually shower in the morning or the evening?"

"Why?" he asked.

"Because I prefer to take a bath in the morning. If you do, too, we'll have to—"

"I'm sharing a bath with you?"

The idea sounded so erotic when he said it that she stifled a small shiver. "I—I hope that won't be too much of a bother."

"It'll be a pleasure," he assured her. "And I'll be happy to shower at night if it'll help."

He was still holding her hand. Anxious to be free of the disturbing feel of his fingers against hers, she tugged loose and looked at her watch. Assuming he would think she was pressed for time, she murmured, "Fine. Now if you'll excuse me? Dinner will be served on the terrace in an hour. I hope that the lovely lake view from your balcony will make up for any inconvenience."

"Do you have a date?" he asked, startling her with the unexpected question.

"What?"

He shrugged his hands into his pockets. "I just wondered if I was making you late for a date."

Her gaze shifted away from his face. "No, just . . . just work."

"Good."

Her gaze went back to meet his; there was a trace of humor in the blue depths. She wondered what he'd meant by "good"? Was he glad he wasn't making her late, or that she didn't have a date?

Was he flirting or wasn't he? The odds were, he was. He was just very subtle about it. But then, why shouldn't he flirt with her? She was female. That would be his only requirement. The story would probably be very different if he'd remembered her—remembered he'd already *had* her. Why did he—of all people in the civilized world—have to show up here, anyway?

Squaring her shoulders, she didn't even attempt a smile. "Have a nice stay, Dr. Redigo."

She'd turned away and was beating a rapid retreat toward the stairs when he reminded softly, "It's Cord... and I plan to."

IT WAS NEARLY ten o'clock and Tess was bone weary when she climbed the stairs to her room. She'd done a decidedly poor job of avoiding Cord. Everywhere she went, she found him. Everywhere she looked, she met his gaze, his dashing smile. After a while even she began to believe she was following him. That was absurd, of course, but if it seemed that way to her, how must it have appeared to him?

Finally she'd resorted to hiding in her office, where she straightened the files for over two hours. Her papers were now so well organized that she'd probably never find anything again for the rest of her life.

Once safe in her room, she decided to go straight to bed. A good night's rest was what she needed. She hurried into the bathroom to get her nightgown, which was hanging beside the tub. She heard the bathroom door click shut behind her before she realized she was not alone.

Though there was no water running in the shower, there was no mistaking the male animal that lurked behind the fogged curtain.

When he heard the clicking of high heels on the tile floor, Cord pulled the clear plastic aside to look out. He'd been rubbing his hair dry with a towel. Sweeping damp, blond strands back from his face, he met her startled gaze, breaking into a grin. "Hello, there."

Tess stood about halfway between the door to her room and the hook that held her nightgown. She didn't know if it would be less embarrassing to make a panicked dash for the exit, or go ahead and get her gown.

While she hesitated, Cord asked, "Did I forget the schedule, or is a back scrub part of the service?"

"I—I'm sorry—I didn't mean to—" She indicated the hook. "My nightgown," she explained weakly.

He looked over at the filmy pink thing and then back at her. "That was my guess, too."

"I'll just get it and go."

There was a merry flicker in his eyes. "Whatever you like."

Wishing she were dead, she snagged the silk gown and backed out, her mind blazing with the slightly hazy view of his well-endowed masculinity. She couldn't help but recall the feel of his virile nakedness so many years ago, when he'd made her body glow with unfamiliar delights.

The experience rattled her, and she lost all desire to sleep. Brooding, disgusted and angry at her wayward train of thought, she decided to take a walk. Her plan was to wear herself out completely.

The night was crisp and cool with a light breeze wafting up from the lake. There was a bright moon, a disk of gold in the black sky. She inhaled, enjoying the night, as she walked down the flagstone path through the well-kept garden of colorful annuals and shrub roses. Low gas lamps lit her way.

When she reached the lawn, she turned back, enjoying the peaceful scene of the darkened Jacobean-style house, soft lights glowing from behind lacy sheers of several second-story guest rooms.

She recalled the first time she'd seen the inn at sunset. What a spectacular sight that had been, the dying sun setting its honey-hewed stone aglow. That had been the only spectacular feature about Lost Cove Inn—aside from its debt.

When she'd come here after her father's death, the old home had been in a state of decay. Her aunt Jewel had recently been widowed and was going blind, and the place was in need of efficient management. Though Tess had been only seventeen, she'd spent a good number of her teen years managing business while her father drank up his salary, so she had gradually taken over running the place. She was proud that, thanks to her management, they'd been able to refurbish the inn and were now on the verge of making a profit.

She scanned the tiled patio, lit by the dim light of one lamp left burning in the drawing room. Virge slouched around dismantling tables while Sugar carried folding chairs toward the kitchen door, bumping and grinding all the way. Having dinner on the patio occasionally had been her idea, and had proved popular with the guests. The extra work hadn't been quite as well received by Virge, but his grumbling was fairly good-natured.

Tess's gaze moved upward. Tall gables graced both ends of the inn. The five chimneys that sprouted from the slate roof were smokeless now. She smiled wryly, hoping that by next winter, when they were billowing smoke again, she wouldn't be.

Her gaze was drawn down to the center section of the inn that bowed out, the second and third stories adorned with wrought-iron balconies. She noticed that Cord's lights were out and assumed he must have gone to bed.

She turned away, her tranquil mood shattered, and headed for the cliffs near the edge of the spruce wood. She escaped there on infrequent nights when concerns of the inn didn't devour all her time. Tonight she really needed to get away.

She sat down cross-legged on the cold stone that jutted out over the lake glistening a hundred feet below. The breeze was a little cool through her cotton blouse; crossing her arms before her, she tried to ignore the chill.

For the first time she saw a ghostly looking cabin cruiser tied up at the inn's dock. Squinting, she could just make out the name. Something Two. "Co-eel—a—can . . . cant—"

"Coelacanth," uttered a disembodied voice that Tess immediately recognized as Cord's. She twisted around, surprised that he could have approached so quietly.

He smiled his uneven smile, and in the moonlight, his teeth shone white, strikingly perfect. "I didn't mean to frighten you, but coelacanth isn't the easiest word to pronounce."

"It's your boat?"

He nodded.

She allowed her eyes one brief trip up and down his trim frame. His thick mane of hair had gone all silvery in the moonlight, and he'd changed into jeans and a white V-necked sweater. It looked like cashmere and it clung like a jealous woman. She wondered a bit peevishly if he had any idea how sexy he looked in the moonlight?

The night of the hayride there had been no moon. She'd hardly been able to see him at all, and look what had happened! Irritation skidded up her spine, and she turned back to face the lake.

Determined not to be affected by him, she wisecracked, "Coelacanth may not be easy to say, but the easy words don't make good boat names. You spend thousands of dollars for a boat, you don't call it Hay." She winced, thinking Freud would have had a field day analyzing that slip of the tongue.

"Hay?" He joined her on the ledge, much to her distress. "As in 'Hey, you' or as in 'bale of hay'?"

She would have given a lot to take back that word. But since she couldn't, she hedged, "You're missing the point."

"I got the point. It's the word choice that fascinates me."

Trying to ignore the fact that his knee grazed her thigh, she countered, "You're easily fascinated."

He was silent for a moment before he asked, "Why are you so nervous?"

She stiffened. "I'm not."

"Oh?" She could tell he was looking directly at her. "Then why are you wringing your hands?"

She hadn't realized that's what she was doing. Dragging her hands apart, she clasped her knees tightly. Damn! She needed a cigarette!

"If it's about the mix-up in the bathroom, forget it."

She clenched her fingers so tightly around her knees that she could feel the imprint of her nails through her slacks. "I wasn't thinking about that at all."

"Then what?"

She turned to face him, exasperated by his doggedness. "Could we change the subject? Some things aren't your business, you know."

A dark eyebrow arched in surprise. For a long moment he said nothing; he simply studied her. When he finally spoke, his voice was lower. "You're right. I apologize."

Her senses were restive. He had a polished, yet endearing charm that was hard to resist. She could detect his cologne, now. It was mellow—an expensive, heady mix.

"I gather you know what it means."

His cryptic remark drew her from her mental wanderings. Confused, she asked, "What?"

"The word 'coelacanth.' Most people ask. Since you didn't I gather you already know."

He'd changed the subject, all right. Unfortunately, she did know what it meant, but she wasn't going to tell him she'd saved the magazine where she'd read about it . . . and him. "What does it mean?"

"It's the name of the fish I'm studying in the Indian Ocean. The coelacanth was thought to be extinct for seventy million years. About fifty years ago it was accidentally discovered. So far, the Indian Ocean is the only body of water where it's been found."

She could tell he was trying to make conversation—trying to make her feel comfortable. Short of leaving the country, she couldn't see any way Cord Redigo could put her at ease. But for the sake of appearances, she faked a relaxed pose. Leaning back on her hands, she scanned the lake where the moon's reflection floated. Though she was dying to ask him to go, she asked instead, "The 'two' in the name means you've only found two fish, I gather."

He chuckled; it was a pleasant sound in the darkness. She'd heard him chuckle before in the dark, though. She swallowed, forcing the memory from her mind as she tried to catch the thread of his conversation. "No, actually this cruiser is the smaller of two that I own. I let Mary use this one most of the time. The big one, *Coelacanth One*, I anchor off the island of Grande Comore, where I do my research."

"Number Two looks pretty big to me."

"It's a twenty-six footer—plenty big to carry the sonar equipment we need. Actually it's good for most everything but sleeping. If you're over five ten it's a little cramped.

She sat up abruptly, fiddling with a strand of her hair. She didn't care to picture this man prone. She switched subjects. "We're all very excited about your research project. Naturally we'd love proof that Champ exists."

"So would Mary. She believes in your mythical monster."

Tess's brow knit in confusion. She turned to scan his profile. The deep cleft in his chin was accentuated by the moonlight. She shook off the quixotic thought that she'd once run her tongue along that deep slash. "You sound like you don't believe in Champ."

He turned to face her. "You're right. I don't."

"You don't?" Unknowingly, she frowned, not sure she'd heard him correctly. "Did you say you don't?"

He shook his head.

She stared at him, incredulous. "You mean you're here to disprove Champ's existence?"

His expression grew earnest. "I'm a marine biologist, a scientist. As far as I'm concerned, Champ is nothing more than a popular piece of local folklore."

"Popular piece of . . . !" She rose to her knees. A nagging little voice told her she was overreacting. He had a right to his opinion. But she'd had a rotten day because of him. She'd had *more* than one rotten day because of him and part of her had waited a very long time to tell him off. "I'll tell you what Champ is. He's our bread and butter, mister!" She emphasized her words with a hearty poke at his chest. "Part and parcel of our identity here on the lake. Most of our guests come here specifically because of Champ." She leaped to her feet. "What are you trying to do, sabotage us?"

Cord stood, too. "No, of course not," he offered gently. "But tell me honestly. Have you ever seen Champ?"

"I don't have to see him to know he's there. Aunt Jewel has, and even now that she's blind, she can still sense when he's near." His indulgent smile did more to fire her anger than any outright argument could have done. "Kalvin has seen him—lots of times."

When he elevated one eyebrow, Tess asserted furiously, "He has!"

Cord started to speak, but she cut him off, lifting a threatening finger. "Don't you dare say anything patronizing or I swear I'll—I'll . . ."

"I know, you'll poke me to death." He smiled wryly at her, drawing her raised hand into his. "I'm not here to disprove Champ's existence. I'm here as a favor to my cousin Mary. She's done a lot for me, and I'd offer to take Bigfoot to the senior prom if she asked me to. But as long as I'm here, I'll look for hard evidence—one way or the other. Truth can't hurt anyone."

Truth can't hurt? There was something about the way he stood there, looking concerned, yet distant. . . . It reminded her of the way he'd looked that night he'd dropped her off at the gas station. Her insides twisted at the reminder and she saw red. "Sometimes, Dr. Redigo, the truth can hurt." She pulled her hand from his. "It can be vicious."

"The last thing I want to do is hurt your business."

"My busi—" She blinked, realizing he was still talking about Champ. He had no idea that she'd been referring to the blunt "truth" he'd told her thirteen years ago when he'd said she was just a kid, unschooled about love—and no doubt lacking sexual skill. That "truth" had hurt her deeply.

His look was intense, questioning as he watched the battle of emotions raging in her face. The concern in his eyes told her that he expected her to explain.

Her heart was thudding dully. There was nothing more she intended to say. Turning abruptly, she hurried away from him, ashamed of her uncharacteristic show of temper. Tomorrow she'd worry about facing him again. But for now, she was going to have to scour the inn for dirty rugs. She needed something to beat.

2

CORD AWOKE when he heard Tess's bathroom door close. Lacing his hands behind his head, he listened to her move around. He recalled the pink nightgown, and found himself picturing her, both in it and out of it. He grinned; it was a bit early in the day for that sort of thinking.

While the bath water ran, he let his imagination conjure up a picture of what she was doing and how she was attired. It passed the time pleasantly enough. Finally, when she turned the water off, he found himself straining to hear her splash as she bathed.

He envisioned her lounging naked in the tub, her olive skin wet and glistening, her sleek black hair twisted into some kind of knot on top of her head, wisps around her face and neck becoming soaked as she soaped her face and shoulders.

She lifted a leg. He didn't know how he knew she lifted a leg, but he did. He closed his eyes.

She had been dressed quite conservatively yesterday, when he'd met her, in beige slacks and a simple blouse that buttoned up to her throat. Even so, the plain clothes didn't completely disguise her lithesome body, nice hips and full round breasts. She was well endowed for a small woman. Of course she wasn't his type at all. He preferred leggy blondes who had all the right equipment and weren't shy about showing it off.

He was far from being a rounder, but when he met someone who gave him a smile that told him she was available, he sometimes accepted the invitation. He always made sure that these brief encounters were understood to be just that; his work took precedence over everything else.

It didn't take Cord long to size up a woman, and he could tell that Tess was not the type who shared herself with a man without the promise of a commitment. He didn't have anything against that. He respected her for her principles. But this time he was a little sorry about it. For a prim woman, Tess had shown a tempting glimmer of passion when she'd lost her temper last night. He'd had an outrageous urge to take her in his arms and savor the heat of it.

His mind snapped back to the present when he heard the slosh of the water as she lifted her other leg. He pictured her soaping her calf, her thigh, then moving on up to soap her stomach and breasts....

He felt a tightening in his gut and rolled out of bed with a low groan. Maybe she wasn't his type, but with the assistance of his greedy imagination, she was showing off all the right equipment. He grinned wryly. If only she knew how his thoughts were running right now, he was sure he'd catch another glimpse of her salty temper.

Rather than listen to her toilette every morning, he decided he'd better plan on being up and gone by—he looked at his watch—six o'clock. There was no point in putting a strain on his . . . imagination. Shaking off a momentary tug of regret that he wouldn't be the man to sample the more pleasant side of Tess's passion, he strolled to his closet. Dragging on a pair of jeans and a soft flannel shirt, he left his room in search of a cup of coffee.

The kitchen was bright, painted a shiny enameled white. Clean and scrubbed, it reminded him of the inn's manager. He inhaled the familiar aroma of breakfast cooking, which conjured up memories of his childhood back in Oklahoma.

Across the kitchen a plump woman was kneading dough, her back to him. She either had a bee up her skirt, or she was doing some sort of pagan fertility dance. He grinned when she burst out singing, "Do—do—do it, baby. . ." She began to sway around in a circle. She'd danced halfway around when she saw him standing there, languidly rolling up his sleeves and smiling. Her round cheeks pinkened. "Oh, hi, there." She pushed the earphones down to her neck. "Can I get you something?"

"Coffee?" He crossed the kitchen in long strides.

"Sure." She scratched her chin with the back of her wrist. "Over by the stove. That big urn. I always have plenty of coffee. The boss likes to have a cup first thing, too." She wiped her floured hands on her apron. "Name's Sugar Smith. Bring me a cup, would you mind? Pottery's in the shelf above."

When Cord had returned with two mugs of steamy coffee, she shook his hand. "And who might you be, handsome?"

He grinned at her forthrightness. "Cord Redigo."

She jerked her head toward a chair near the corner. A rotund man was asleep there, his head lolled back, his mouth gaping open. "That's my sweetie pie, Virge. He's taking a break. Had a busy night." She nudged Cord in the ribs. "If you get my drift."

Her enthusiasm was infectious. Cord chuckled. Apparently there was an energetic side to Virge that wasn't apparent at the moment. He said, "I have a feeling Virge is a lucky man."

His remark surprised and delighted her. She hooted, "Well, now, a good-looker and a smooth-talker, too. Mighty sassy combination in a big boy," she said, nudging him once more before taking up her kneading. "Just don't try to get your pretty hooks into me. I'm taken." She grinned as she flipped the wad of dough over.

"Spoilsport," he teased.

She laughed. "My Virge is all the man I can handle. Ya know, they say the way to a man's heart is through his stomach. Well, to tell you the truth, I was a little plain when I was younger. That's why I became a cook. Wanted to get a man to love me for my grub. But now that I'm older and wiser, well—" she leaned nearer to him and nodded knowingly "—that stomach jazz is a bunch of potato peelings. There's only one sure-fire way to a man's heart, and that's got nothing to do with the kitchen, if you get my drift."

He braced himself for her nudge this time, then teased, "I don't know. I've heard rumors that wild things can go on in kitchens."

She guffawed. "Well, me and Virge can't very well chase each other around in here dressed in our birthday suits. There's health department codes, you know."

"You're probably right," Cord remarked, hiding a grin behind the rim of his coffee cup.

"Oh, hi, boss." Sugar waved, and Cord glanced around to see Tess coming down the stairs. He smiled at her. She smiled back, but the gesture seemed a little forced. He was drawn back to Sugar when she said in an aside, "Come by later, I always keep a couple of extra cinnamon rolls for big, good-looking boys."

"Doesn't Virge get jealous?" Cord asked, with mock concern.

"My sweetie pie knows I only have eyes for him—it's just cinnamon rolls I got for you." She nudged him again. "But they're darned good cinnamon rolls."

"Thanks. I'll remember." He glanced back at Virge and decided the snoring man had a treasure in his wife.

Lounging against the counter, he took a sip of his coffee and enjoyed the view of Tess walking to the urn and pouring herself coffee. Something about her tugged at his memory. He'd noticed it yesterday, but the feeling had been indistinct. Now the feeling was back. Where had he seen her before?

She was dressed in green slacks and a green blouse, the same emerald color as her eyes. The slacks were slightly baggy, which was the style, Cord realized. It was at times like this when he wondered what strange, asexual notions went through some designers' minds.

Her blouse looked like silk. Though it was oversize, when she walked it molded to her curves, hiding nothing. He doubted she was aware of that.

She turned to face him, taking a sip of her coffee. This morning she had her hair parted in the middle and tied at her neck with a green ribbon. Very few women could wear their hair pulled back so severely and still look feminine and soft. But Tess, with her dark subtle beauty, managed to carry it off.

He was especially attracted to her high, handsome cheekbones, full lips, and exotically shaped, green eyes. Whenever Cord caught her looking his way, those eyes slightly narrowed, he was reminded of an aloof, haughty cat studying her prey. He smiled to himself at the crazy thought.

She seemed to be struggling with some problem this morning; her gaze held an odd, penetrating quality as she peered at him over the rim of her coffee cup. He decided to break the ice and smiled encouragingly. "Sleep well?"

His remark seemed to help her make a decision. She walked over to him. "Dr. Redigo," she began, setting her cup beside his on the counter.

"Cord," he reminded.

"Yes, well." She angled her head up, looking poised but slightly pained. "I hope you'll forgive me for my uncalled-for remarks last night."

He lifted a brow. So that was it. "Forget it. You only said what you felt."

"I was wrong. I shouldn't have given you trouble just because you don't believe in Champ. I had no right to get so . . . so snippy."

He pursed his lips to hide a smile. Snippy? Perhaps a bit of an understatement, but a quaint word. He decided it was probably just as well that she never know how her heated outburst had affected him. Nodding as seriously as he could, he assured her, "No apology necessary. You just echoed what Mary told me—that if I give her any guff, she'll tan my backside the way she did when I was little." He smiled kindly. "I really don't want to be your enemy, Tess."

Her eyes widened, and for the life of him, he couldn't figure out why. She fumbled for her coffee cup and put it to her lips, mumbling, "Look, I've got to take breakfast out to my aunt. Will you wait here? I want you to talk to someone."

"I'll be here," he promised.

She nodded and busied herself outfitting a tray. She pointedly avoided eye contact with him, and after a few hurried minutes gathering toast, juice, jam, coffee and a vase with one carnation, she pushed through the kitchen door and was gone. He watched the door swing back and forth in her wake, intrigued by what could possibly be making her so edgy.

To Tess, the sound of her heels striking the freshly buffed oak floor of the reception room seemed unusually loud. She was struggling with the knob on the patio door when she became aware of a tingling at her nape. Sensing someone's presence, she turned slightly and discovered that Cord was standing behind her.

"Let me get that for you," he offered with a smile. It was that damnable, crooked smile that always managed to turn her bones into underdone custard. *The devil take that smile,* she raged inwardly. But outwardly, she appeared placid and businesslike—she hoped.

His hand grazed hers on the knob. As she shifted the tray in her arms, she could still feel a warm sensation where his fingers had brushed hers.

He twisted the knob.

"It sticks," she explained. "If you press down, just a little—"

He had the door opened before she could finish. Motioning her through, he said, "I didn't think you'd mind my meeting your aunt?"

She slid by him, inhaling his cologne. He smelled awfully good in the morning, she noted, filing away the information with other "Cord Redigo tidbits" that some obstinate part of her brain insisted on hoarding. "I'm sure my aunt would love to meet you. She's very gregarious," Tess offered, working at being conversational.

He chuckled. "I like that in an aunt."

She peered back over her shoulder, wondering if he was making fun of her. He smiled pleasantly. She decided he was just being conversational, too.

There were already several guests out on the patio, enjoying the view of the glistening lake.

"She's the regal lady nearest the hedge of yellow roses, wearing the white dress and wide-brimmed hat."

"She looks like something out of a Victorian novel."

"She does," Tess agreed with a loving smile. "She's a very young fifty, and one of the sweetest women I know. But don't let her demure looks fool you. She'll tell you exactly what's on her mind."

"I gather you taught her everything you know," he remarked softly. "I'll like her."

Tess glanced up at him. A grin slow-danced across his crooked, sexy mouth. She lowered her eyes, feeling awkward and tongue-tied. She didn't appreciate idle flattery.

"That was a compliment," he assured her.

"I recognized it for what it was," she returned a bit brusquely. "Aunt Jewel," she called, determined to put an end to his teasing.

At the sound of her name, Jewel turned, the wide brim of her hat fluttering in the breeze. She smiled, and held out a long, thin hand in greeting. Her smile was bright, her sightless eyes hidden behind large, square sunglasses. "Tess, darling." She beckoned her niece forward. "You're early. I hadn't expected you for—"

"I couldn't sleep," Tess broke in, deciding the truth wouldn't seem particularly significant to Cord. "I hope you're hungry."

"Famished, my dear. You know I can always root like a veritable pig...." She paused, her smile increasing slightly. "And who is the delicious-smelling gentleman with you?"

Tess placed the tray on the white iron table. She wasn't surprised at her aunt's ability to detect Cord's presence. As a matter of fact, she wouldn't have been surprised had her aunt said, Who's the sexy hunk sending out the animal vibrations? Before she could reply, Cord stepped forward and took her aunt's hand. "I'm Cord Redigo, a newly arrived guest."

"Ah, well, Mr. Redigo," she placed her other hand over his. "It is certainly a pleasure to meet you. I'm Jewel McCoy Armstrong, Tess's mother's sister."

"A pleasure, ma'am."

Jewel laughed lightly. "Ma'am? Do I detect a cowboy in our midst?"

"Maybe, once," he corrected with a grin.

"You have a very rich voice. Are you a country singer, by any chance?"

His chuckle sent a pleasant sensation up Tess's back. "No, ma'am. For the most part, I only sing in the shower. I'm a marine biologist."

She had withdrawn her hands from his and was adjusting a silver curl at her forehead when she stopped, frowning in thought. "A marine biologist, you say?"

The question triggered panic in Tess. She'd forgotten her aunt's sharp memory. She'd also forgotten she'd read her aunt *the* article.

When Cord assured her that he was, Jewel asked, "I thought the name Redigo rang a bell. Are you Dr. Cordell Redigo, the marine biologist studying the—oh, the name of the fish escapes me, but it's in the Indian Ocean. Am I right?"

Cord's brows lifted with surprise. "Coelacanth. You're quite knowledgeable about a rather obscure subject."

Jewel laughed. "You flatter me, Doctor. But about you—why is a scientist of such international stature gracing our small inn with a visit?"

Cord smiled ruefully. "I don't know about international stature, but I came to New York to deliver the first two live specimens of the coelacanth to the New York Aquarium."

"The first live specimens?" Jewel clasped her hands together in delight. "Why, that's history-making, Dr. Redigo. I congratulate you." She waved a hand. "But I interrupted you. Why have you come here?"

"I decided that I was so close, I'd spend a little time with my cousin, Mary. She was coming here so I joined her and her team of cryptozoologists searching for evidence of Champ."

He cast Tess a brief glance. There was an assurance in his gaze that told her he wouldn't tell her aunt that he doubted their monster's existence.

"Evidence of Champ? Oh, how wonderful. I certainly wish you luck, Dr. Redigo."

Tess gritted her teeth.

"Call me Cord," he offered. His eyes had flicked momentarily to Tess. He hadn't missed her grimace. She couldn't be sure, but it looked as if his lips had twitched at her distress. He was asking, "Tell me, Jewel, how do you know so much about my work?"

Tess closed her eyes, feeling sick. She had no way to signal her aunt not to tell him how she knew.

Meanwhile, Jewel's laughter rang merrily across the patio. She fanned the air with her fingers, searching for Tess's hand. "Why, my niece read an article about you to me several months ago, didn't you, dear? You see, my late husband was a naturalist. I simply love scientists—and poetry. Along with my favorite sonnets, Tess reads me the *Smithsonian* and the *Geographic* every month. You remember that article, don't you, dear?"

Caught like a mouse with her cheeks full of cheese, Tess pestered her lower lip nervously. Cord had turned to look at her and there was little she could do but face him. She did, with regret. He was openly studying her. "I—I suppose so. I'd forgotten," she said, deliberately withdrawing her gaze from his quizzical expression. "You have a wonderful memory, Aunt Jewel."

She laughed, "And you have a wonderful grip. I believe my fingers are breaking."

"Oh..." Tess hadn't realized that in her anxiety she'd tightened her hold on her aunt's hand. She let go. "I'm sorry."

"No harm done." With a dismissive wave, she placed her hands on the edge of her tray. "Dr. Redigo, Tess, I'd love for you to join me for breakfast."

"Maybe some other time, Aunt Jewel," Tess declined for them both. She was highly agitated, afraid her aunt would come up with details about the article that would make it even harder for Cord to believe she had no memory of it. "Dr. Redigo needs to talk to someone about Champ."

"Ah, yes." She nodded. "He must be about his business. Our Champ is very important to us. Once again, good fortune in your search."

"Thank you," Cord replied, taking Tess's arm and moving away with her.

As soon as they were out of earshot, she whispered, "Don't ever let her know you don't believe in Champ. It would break her heart."

He turned to face her after he'd closed the patio door. "I have no intention of breaking anyone's heart."

She grew suddenly irritated. "The road to hell is paved with good intentions, Dr. Redigo."

His eyes wandered over her taut body while she fumed silently. Finally, he asked, "What does that mean?"

"It means..." She faltered, wanting to scream *It means you may not intend to break hearts, but you do!* She swallowed, calming herself. "It means you'll break my aunt's heart if you disprove Champ's existence—whether you intend to or not."

His eyes narrowed. There was something in his look that made her nervous. "Why did you pretend you'd never heard of me?"

She was taken completely off guard by his question and inhaled sharply. "Why...I...never..."

He waited, watching her closely. He would have made a great police interrogator, she thought. He had a very intimidating stare. But *she* had a very disquieting secret to hide, and a medieval torture chamber could not have dragged it out of her. Sighing heavily, she put a hand to the back of a small, unimportant lie and shoved it forward. "My aunt has a better memory for trivia than I do, that's all." She lifted her chin, almost daring him to doubt her.

"I see," he replied evenly. There was no humor in his eyes now. "I suppose most of the world would consider the study of an obscure throwback of marine life trivial." He took her arm, leading her away from the door. "Thank you for clearing that up."

Was it possible that she had pricked this man's ego? Hurt his feelings? It had never occurred to her that he was reachable in that way. If she had injured his pride, it didn't make her feel particularly proud of herself.

But neither did it make her feel bad enough to tell him the truth.

"Where are we going?" he asked, bringing her abruptly back to the present.

"Oh." She looked around. She hadn't been paying much attention to where they were going. She'd only been aware of the solemn look on his face before he'd turned away, and the gentle persuasion of his hand at her elbow. "Out behind the guest cottages. Kalvin is weeding the ground cover."

"Kalvin?"

"Yes, Kalvin. He's sighted Champ many times. I think you should talk to him."

"Oh, you do?" He sounded doubtful.

Her gaze flew to his. "Yes, I do," she shot back. "Or would eyewitness sightings put a crimp in your skepticism?"

Either he winced, or anger created a tic in his jaw. She couldn't tell.

"You don't like me much, do you?" he said, his eyes holding hers.

The remark startled her, and her righteous anger faded. She lowered her eyes feeling unaccountably flustered. "Don't be silly, Dr. Redigo. Surely you've run into people who disagreed with you before."

When he didn't speak for a moment, she met his gaze again. He lifted one brow. It was a very expressive movement, telling her he wasn't buying. "You haven't liked me from the first moment I walked into the kitchen yesterday."

Her breath stopped momentarily as she looked into those azure depths. When she couldn't bear the intensity of his gaze one instant longer, she pivoted away, heading down the corridor. "That's an absurd idea," she lied. "Just because a woman doesn't throw herself at you, you think she hates you? You must have quite an ego, Dr. Redigo."

"And that's another thing," he added, following her into the kitchen, past Sugar and out the back door. "You insist this place is one big family, and you have yet to call me Cord."

"It's a hard name to remember." She changed the subject abruptly. "The cottages are on the edge of the spruce woods," she said, indicating the direction with a brisk wave. Two quaint cottages were barely visible among the evergreens. "Kalvin should be around back."

He said nothing else until they were behind the small guest houses. There Kalvin was, on his knees, weeding the blue-leafed hosta.

"Kal, I want you to tell Dr. Redigo about your Champ sightings."

The young handyman clumsily got to his feet, dusting his grimy gardening gloves on his overalls. "Huh?" he asked, his gaze flying from her to the tall man by her side.

"Tell Dr. Redigo about your eyewitness sightings. He's here to find out about Champ." She smiled at Kalvin as encouragingly as she could under the circumstances. "He wants to know what you've seen."

"Oh." Kalvin gave Cord a gap-toothed grin. "Sure." He peeled off the gloves and dropped them in the wheelbarrow where he'd been dumping the weeds. "I seen ol' Champ lots of times." His face became clouded by a slight frown. "You gonna take notes, or what?"

Cord smiled kindly at the young man and remarked, "I have a good memory, Kalvin. Go ahead."

Tess watched the two men as Kalvin talked. After a few minutes she began to feel less angry and stiff. She had to give Cord credit. He appeared genuinely interested in what Kalvin had to say, giving no indication that he doubted one word. He nodded knowingly several times. It almost appeared to Tess that he considered Kalvin a scientific equal.

She felt fairly relaxed after about ten minutes. Cord had asked pertinent questions and apparently accepted Kalvin's answers with interest and even respect.

"I swear," Kalvin said, slapping his hands together for emphasis, "Ol' Champ's back humped up above the surface. I seen that lots of times. But he was gone too quick for me to get my camera." He scraped his fingers through his hair in his excitement until the straggly strands stood straight up.

"I see, Kalvin. Well, that should give me something to go on, at least." Cord extended a hand. "I appreciate your input."

Kalvin rubbed his palm on his overalls before accepting the doctor's hand. "Sure, thing, Cord. Any ol' time. I get off work at suppertime."

"Thanks. I'll remember." He gave Tess a glance that told her he was ready to leave. When they were some distance away, he said curtly, "I've got a meeting with Mary and the others at eight o'clock. If you don't have any more interviews for me right now, I'd like to have breakfast."

She caught the edge in his voice, and felt a tinge of guilt for having given him such a bad time this morning. She'd softened a little in the last quarter hour, watching him with Kalvin. It had brought back memories of the Cord Redigo she'd first heard about in high school. A nice guy. Everybody'd liked him. Through all these years filled with resentment, she'd forgotten that had been part of her original attraction to him.

She'd also admired the way he'd listened, the way he asked questions. There'd been something substantial there—a good mind at work. That, too, had been one of the things that she'd liked about him so long ago. There had been more to him than just his striking good looks. There still was.

She managed a shy smile, falling into step beside him as he left the wooded area. "That wasn't such a waste of time, was it?"

When he met her gaze, there was just a shadow of a frown on his face. "No more than I expected."

She stared, surprised. "What do you mean? He had some very convincing evidence, I thought."

"Tess," he remarked softly, but firmly, "he was describing an eight-foot sturgeon rolling on the surface, driftwood caught in a current, a deer swimming across the cove in a fog. This sort of mistaken sighting isn't unusual. Especially for a monster hysteric like Kalvin. You tell some people there's a monster in a glass of water and they'll see one. I'm afraid Kalvin isn't a very reliable witness. He wants to see Champ too badly."

"But you acted like you believed him," she charged. "Surely you can't discount every—"

"Ms Mankiller?" Kalvin called from the edge of the woods. "Want me to pick them bouquets of sweet william for the cottages? Them honeymooners is comin' tonight."

Tess's panic revved into high gear. It had only taken her a surreptitious glance at Cord to know that the name had struck a cord in his memory.

Her heart ramming her ribs like a bulldozer, she tried to answer Kalvin with something sensible. The honest truth was, at this horrible moment, she didn't care if he picked bouquets of sweet william or threw poison ivy through the cottage windows.

With a tremulous smile, she nodded. "Yes. That'll be fine, Kalvin, just fine. . . ." When he'd ambled back into the trees, she edged away, hoping to make her escape without speaking to Cord. She wasn't ready to meet his gaze—his damnable, knowing gaze.

She'd only made it a few steps when he swore, hauling her around to face him. "I knew we'd met. Good Lord! You're the . . . virgin." The last word had come out in a whisper, sounding as if he'd dragged it through a lot of pain to get it said.

She wished she were at the bottom of Lake Champlain, her humiliation was so total. Her throat had gone dry as Oklahoma dust and her eyes stung. Feeling frightened and hurt, she mumbled bitterly, "You should be the last person on earth to call me that."

His eyes, shades darker, clung to her as she suffered in silence. "I can't believe you're here. After that summer, I never expected to see you again. Where did you go?"

She tugged her arms from his grasp. "What does it matter now? It didn't interest you then." His image was shimmering, blurry. She grew furious with herself for allowing him to see her tears and turned away.

It surprised her when he stepped in front of her, blocking her escape. He touched her cheeks, tipping her face up to meet his solemn eyes. "It mattered. I worried about you . . . whether you got pregnant—"

She swung her hand automatically, an act of pure passion. But he was fast. He caught her wrist in a gentle grip and halted her fingers just inches from his cheek. Muttering a curse that was ripe with self-loathing, he asked, "You didn't get pregnant, did you?"

Her chest constricted and she felt as if she were choking. "Take your hands off me," she warned coldly.

When he reluctantly obliged, she ground out, "No, I didn't. I hope that ties up any loose ends. . . ." She pushed past him.

"Let me explain one thing—please."

There was something so compelling in his request that she found herself coming to an unsteady halt. Refusing to turn and face him, she rasped, "I'm listening."

"I had to leave town the next morning. Mary got me a spot on a research project in the Galapagos Islands. It was the chance of a lifetime for a kid just out of high school. I was gone for three weeks." He paused. When he spoke again, his voice was low and rough with emotion. "I looked for you, Tessa Jane. No one knew where Joe Mankiller and his daughter had gone." She felt his fingers curl around her wrist. "I've thought about you a lot since then."

She jerked back from his touch, her ribbon falling away to leave her hair flying wildly about her as she stumbled away from him. "I'll just bet you have!" she cried. "I'll bet it's given you plenty of great laughs with the boys in the bunkhouse!"

Her angry, pain-filled eyes stabbed his for only a brief moment, but long enough to wound. The white-hot blade of her fury seared through him, making him wince.

"Now you know why I don't like you very much, *Dr.* Redigo!"

She whirled away, and blinded by fury and tears, barely missed plowing into a tall, slender woman who had just come out of the kitchen door. The newcomer was attractive, with a no-nonsense head of graying curls. She gave Tess a startled smile and said, "Why, hello, I'm Mary Cash. Remember me? We met briefly last night at dinner."

Tess tried valiantly to rein in her temper. This was Cord's zoologist cousin. The one who believed in Champ. Unfortunately, there was a bit too much family resemblance in her smile to satisfactorily quell Tess's rage. Drawing a harsh breath, she managed, "Yes, of course, Dr. Cash—Mary—er, if you'll excuse me, I really need to—"

"Is anything wrong, Miss Mankiller? You seem upset." Mary's smile wilted a little.

"It's really nothing," Tess mumbled, running a jerky hand through her hair.

Mary's gaze drifted beyond Tess's shoulder. She spotted Cord, standing some twenty feet away, his expression grim.

Encompassing both of them with a curious look, she said, "Well, I see you've been chatting with my cousin." Obviously trying to ease the tension that hung in the air, she quipped, "Darling Cord doesn't usually make a woman this angry until he dumps her."

Gritting her teeth against a curse, Tess remarked shortly, "A fine old Redigo tradition, no doubt. If you'll pardon me, I must..." She muttered something she hoped sounded rational and hurried away. She didn't give a damn where she was going, all she knew was that she wanted to be as far away from Cord Redigo as the local geography would allow.

Mary watched Tess retreat into the inn before turning back to stare at Cord.

"Well..." She walked over to him, eyeing him suspiciously. "Making new friends, I see."

A long silence followed as Cord stood there, images of the young Tessa Jane of his past racing through his brain. The hurt that had glittered in her green eyes when he'd left her standing in that dimly lit gas station was the same dreadful torment he'd seen a moment ago—still raw, still as fresh and stormy as that night so long ago, when... He suddenly realized his cousin had spoken to him. "What?" he growled.

"Whoa, don't bark at me. I'm the innocent bystander here," Mary chided, touching his jaw. "Why the heavy-duty tic, Cord? What exactly did she mean by 'a fine old Redigo tradition'? You two know each other before yesterday?"

He glanced at his cousin through half-lowered lids. Her bright blue eyes were wide with curiosity. Snorting derisively, he said, "You're a busybody, you know that?"

She pinched his cheek. "Maybe. But I know you, kid, and I ask again. Did you know the lady before?"

He shrugged. "Briefly. In high school."

"Well, it appears the acquaintance wasn't brief enough. What did you do to her?"

Cord passed his cousin a jaundiced look. "I don't appreciate your assumption that I did anything to her."

"Well, did you or didn't you?"

He exhaled heavily. "I suppose I did."

"You brute!" She cuffed his arm with her fist. "What, exactly, did you do?" Her worried face was tilted up, expectant.

"Mary?" With a humorless chuckle, he draped an arm around her shoulders. "May I make a suggestion?"

She sighed as he dragged her toward the kitchen door.

"If you must."

"Mind your own damned business."

3

MARY TURNED AROUND and stared down at Cord as he followed her up the long wooden staircase from the dock to the inn's lawn. "You outta breath, big fella?"

He frowned up at her. "What?"

"I said, are you—"

"I heard what you said," he interrupted. "Do I look out of breath?"

She shrugged. "Not really. But you look...weird."

He laughed without humor. "And people say you have no tact."

"Who says that?" she asked, her eyes flashing with mischief.

"Mainly me—sometimes Jack."

"Oh, pooh. What do cousins and husbands know?" Taking his arm, she walked with him up the remainder of the stairs. "No, really, Cord. You've been preoccupied all day. Why, you hardly said a word to the other team members while we were out on mid-lake surveillance."

"It's hard to engage in sparkling conversation, drive the boat and watch the sonar chart recorder at the same time," Cord reminded her evenly.

"Hard? For you?" Her laughter was quick. "Cord, dear, you could charm the pants off a roomful of scientific types, write a research paper and teach a college level course in ichthyology all at the same time if you had a mind to. I've seen you do it."

He grunted. "To paraphrase Shakespeare, Mary, you're full of bull."

"That's the first line of Shakespeare I've ever understood." She laughed through the words. "No, seriously. Is your lousy mood because of what happened between you and the manager this morning?"

He slanted her a narrowed glance. "Her name's Tess."

Mary nodded. "I know her name. But her name's not the point. Is it?"

He looked away. The inn rose before them, glowing brilliantly in the reflected sunset. "No. Her name's not the point."

"Well, what is, then?"

They'd reached the top of the stairs. Cord turned to face his cousin and smiled wearily. "The point is, I hurt her badly. I didn't mean to, but I did, and . . ."

"And you feel like the back end of a horse about it. And rightfully so," she added helpfully.

"You know, Mary. You should hire yourself out to salt wounds."

She sniffed, ignoring his gibe. "Are you going to tell her you feel like a jerk? I mean, after all, you'll be bumping into her a lot in the next month. You ought to try to make amends."

He exhaled slowly. "It won't be easy. She doesn't want to talk to me."

Mary nodded. "I noticed. Well—" She swatted him on his backside. "No time like the present, kiddo. I'll check on the shore surveillance team while you go eat crow."

Apparently she thought that was all that needed to be said on the subject. Cord shook his head at her retreating form. Thin and erect, tart yet tender, Mary was more than a cousin to him. Ten years his senior, she was like a big sister, always mother-henning him. It didn't look as if she had any plans to stop.

He turned toward the inn, striking in the setting sun. But at this moment, he could see only angry tears glistening in narrowed green eyes, and bright black hair swirling about the sweet, anguished face of Tessa Jane Mankiller.

He hoped he could get her to stand still long enough for him to tell her how much he regretted what he'd done that night so long ago, how many times he'd berated himself for it over the years and how often he'd wondered what had happened to her. It would be one of the most belated apologies on record, but it would be no less sincere.

He looked at his watch. It was after seven. He had no idea where she might be, so he decided to check at the front desk.

The double doors to the patio were slightly ajar. When he stepped through them into the reception hall, he found himself staring at a couple clutched in an embrace. He felt momentarily anxious. A man, tall and slender, and dressed like a banker, was holding Tess to him, kissing her. Cord frowned to see the long, glorious mass of her hair entrapped within a stranger's arms.

He hadn't expected this. But why wouldn't she have a lover? Just because her name was still Mankiller didn't mean there were no men in her life.

The kiss didn't go on long, but still Cord chafed at having to watch. It wasn't his habit to indulge in voyeurism. A little acidly, he reminded himself that they were the ones who had chosen such a public place for their little show of passion, not him. He glanced away, trying to concentrate on the nineteenth-century bird prints that were hung on the paneled walls.

The stranger's throaty sigh drew Cord's attention in spite of himself. When Tess and her companion realized they were being watched, they separated immediately. Cord heard Tess's breathy gasp as she moved away to straighten her clothes.

Cord's grin was deceptive in its pleasantness. He hoped the sudden irritation he felt wouldn't color his words. "Excuse me, folks. Didn't mean to intrude. . . ." He began to move toward the hallway that led to the kitchen, having decided that now would not be the best time to engage Tess in a conversation about the night they'd made love thirteen years ago. Before he'd taken two steps, cool fingers brushed his wrist, stopping him.

"Oh, Dr. Redigo." Tess smiled up at him. It was a valiant effort, Cord decided, but not very convincing. Her lips trembled slightly at their upturned corners. "I'd like you to meet a close friend of mine. Nolan Lamont. He's the inn's CPA."

The slim, impeccably dressed stranger held out his hand. As Cord accepted it, he noticed the excellent cut of his tweed sports coat, the maroon-and-navy striped silk tie, snowy shirt, navy trousers and unscuffed oxfords. The man shouted conservatism. Cord hadn't pictured Tessa Jane Mankiller with that type. He'd always seen her with Indy race-car drivers or one of the air force's Blue Angels or . . . He shook off the curious realization that he had, over the years, wondered about the type of man little Tessa Jane Mankiller would end up with. Nolan Lamont, the CPA, had not been one of them.

"How do you do, Doctor," Nolan said. "Tess tells me you're up here to search for Champ." He smiled and dropped his hand.

As Cord nodded, he scanned the man's face. He was nice-looking in a quiet sort of way. His face was long and thin, his forehead high, his dark brown hair very curly and cropped close to his head.

"Do you expect to find him?" Before Cord had a chance to answer Nolan's question, the other man laughed. It was a rather high-pitched chortle. "Tess and I have gone around and around on that subject." He squeezed her shoulders lovingly. "Haven't we, dear?"

Tess's gaze, which had hovered uncertainly around the edges of Cord's face, fluttered up to meet her companion's eyes. "What?"

His smile faded a bit. "I said, you and I've disagreed on the existence of Champ over the years."

"Oh, yes." She looked back at Cord, her face going a little stiffer. "You see, Dr. Redigo, you're not the only doubter among us."

"Oh?" Nolan asked, interested. "You doubt our local monster's existence, too? I wouldn't have thought so, since you're here with a search team."

Tess's boyfriend was toying with the lace collar of her blouse. There was something disquieting about his familiarity with her. Cord couldn't fathom why he'd feel either protective or possessive of the petite woman. There was no earthly reason why he should. Still, he wished Nolan would slack off on the public stroking. It was annoying.

He lifted his gaze to Tess's eyes. Her look was guarded. She seemed so small and vulnerable that he decided not to add to her distress, saying only, "Reality can be every bit as charming as fairy tales. I see no reason to form armed camps either way."

Nolan chuckled. "Well put. Don't you think so, Tess?"

She was looking at Cord with what appeared to be complete and utter loathing. After a pause that was a little too long, she bit out, "Sometimes reality can let you down."

Cord felt the sting of her words, but his gaze held hers steadily.

Nolan looked down at her, remarking, "Now that's an odd thing to say." He rested his hand on her shoulder, his fingers grazing the barest rise of her breast. Nolan was certainly flaunting his proprietorship. To be honest, Cord couldn't blame Nolan. Tess was lovely.

"And just how has reality let my little Tess down?" Nolan queried gently.

She shook her head and smiled wanly up at him. "Never mind. It's not important."

Cord's mood had been bad all day, and it was getting no better watching the mating dance between these two. He decided to get the hell out of there. His smile was deceptively charming. "Call me Cord, Nolan." He looked down at Tess, adding, "You, too, Miss Mankiller. I thought I mentioned that before."

Pride lifted her chin slightly before she replied, "Perhaps you did. I don't recall."

"I know it's a difficult name." He peered at her thoughtfully. "Think about rope—a hangman's noose. That might help."

She tossed her head in a haughty gesture. "It might."

"And I'm Nolan to my friends," the other man offered, completely unaware of the tension sizzling in the room.

Cord nodded. "Thanks. Well, I think I'll go clean up for dinner." He looked down at Tess. "Or will you be needing the bathroom?"

She appeared surprised by the unexpected change of subjects. "I—no. Feel free."

With a brief nod, he turned to go, but was halted when Tess called, "Oh, by the way... Cord?"

He looked back over his shoulder, surprised to hear her use his first name. "Yes?"

She moved out from under Nolan's arm, taking a step toward him. She seemed apprehensive. "I was hoping..." She clasped her hands together before her. "What I mean is, usually Nolan has the room you're using when he drops in. I was wondering if you'd mind sharing it with him. We'd roll in another bed, of course. You see, with room twelve out and all..." She wet her lips and waited.

Nolan leaped into the breach. "If it would be a bother, I'm sure I could get Kalvin to put me up."

Cord hid his surprise that Nolan and Tess were not sharing her bed. Slowly, a grin spread over his face. "No problem, Nolan. Be my guest." When he turned away, he was still smiling. So Tess wasn't sleeping with Nolan Lamont. He cocked a speculative brow.

NOLAN HELD THE DOOR for Tess as they headed out on the darkened patio. She stifled a yawn. It had been a long, stressful day for her, and this surprise visit from Nolan was taking its toll.

"You're not tired, are you?" Nolan asked.

She took his arm. "A little. It's getting late...."

He chuckled, walking her toward a vacant table. "Nonsense. Didn't you promise me a round of bridge?"

"Oh, but Nolan, the game of charades took longer than I thought it would," she said. "And besides, even with that biology teacher—Fred something—we don't have a fourth."

"I play."

Tess straightened. Cord's voice had come from the shadow of a twisted old apple tree that stood at the edge of the patio. Her eyes had adjusted to the darkness by now, and she could just make him out. His lean, sinewy form was draped casually against the crooked trunk. It occurred to Tess that if he could have found a straw, he'd have been chewing on it.

He cocked his head in mute greeting. "Didn't mean to eavesdrop. Just came out here to enjoy the breeze off the lake."

"Why, hello, Cord," Nolan said with a friendly smile. "Missed you at charades. Tess, here, is a master of mime. She can say more with her expressions than most people can with a full dictionary at their disposal."

Cord ducked under a low limb and ambled over, lanky and in control. Her world teetered slightly. She wanted to run.

"Is that so?" he asked, a parody of a grin flickering across his lips.

Tess heard the sarcasm in his words. She forced her frozen lips to curve into a semblance of a smile, matching his, counterfeit for counterfeit. "I gather you're not much for group activities," she remarked archly, her nerves wound taut again. Why could she never be around this man without feeling as though she was standing on live electric wires?

"Depends on the group," he drawled. "I gather your team won."

Nolan hugged Tess to him. "Naturally. So you play bridge, Cord?"

"Sometimes."

"Great, then we have a fourth. Why don't I go round up Fred and grab us a pot of coffee?" He gave Tess a quick peck on the cheek. "See you two in five."

Tess's sigh was audible when he had gone.

"Anything wrong?"

She turned back to face him, blurting, "No. Of course not. Do you—do you happen to have a cigarette?"

"I don't smoke." He crossed his arms across his chest. "And you shouldn't, either."

"Please," she exhaled tiredly. "Don't lecture me."

"Sorry."

He didn't sound particularly sorry. She turned toward the lake and was surprised to see two figures walking up the garden path. One was unmistakably her Aunt Jewel. The other, a man, she couldn't place. Jewel was holding the man's arm. More to herself than Cord, she whispered, "Who in the world is that?"

"Quillan Quimby. He's a retired English professor, here with his granddaughter, and a member of the Champ search team. It seems both Jewel and Quillan have an abiding love for John Donne's poetry." Cord chuckled.

She smiled in spite of her mood, watching the couple's leisurely approach. "He must be a nice man."

"Liking John Donne makes a man nice in your book?"

Casting him a disdainful look, she said, "It shows a certain degree of sensitivity, yes." She turned away, but not too soon to see the glint of his teeth. Why was he grinning at her? He was such an irritating man!

"I see," he remarked quietly. After a brief pause, he began,

Goe and catche a falling stare,
Get with child a mandrake roote,
Tell me, where all past yeares are,

Or who cleft the Divels foot,
Teach me to heare Mermaides singing . . .

Tess turned back to stare at him as he watched her. His expression now solemn, he recited John Donne just above a whisper,

Or to keep off envies stinging,
And finde
What winde
Serves to advance an honest minde . . .

He pursed his lips. "Shall I go on?"

She shot him a withering look and turned away. Why did he have to thwart her at every turn? "Don't bother." She said the words slowly, watching her aunt and the white-haired stranger approach. "You proved your point."

"Just what point did I prove?"

"That even ax murderers can memorize poetry. Maybe I'd better go check out this Quillan Quimby." She stalked away from him, heading toward her aunt. When she reached the couple, Quillan was assisting her aunt up the step to the patio. "Aunt Jewel," she said, taking her aunt's free hand. "I thought that was you."

"Oh, Tess, dear, what a lovely surprise." Jewel's voice lilted with laughter. "I want you to meet Quillan Quimby, recently retired professor of Elizabethan and Jacobean poetry from the English department at the University of Vermont in Burlington. Is he not a gift sent from heaven?"

"Well—I—yes, he certainly seems so. Mr. Quimby—" Tess shook his hand "—Dr. Redigo was just telling me how much you like John Donne."

The professor, tall and thin, with the good looks of a silver-haired Cary Grant, pressed his fingers around Tess's with a warmth as friendly and gentle as his smile. "How do you do, Tess," he said, his voice strong, yet slightly raspy. "Your aunt has done nothing but sing your praises."

Tess laughed nervously. "Well, I certainly hope your next walk will involve more interesting conversation."

Quillan squeezed her fingers before releasing her hand. "On the contrary. She was explaining your wonderful name—Mankiller. She tells me that you are half Cherokee Indian. You see, I'm a thirty-second Shawnee, myself. And—" he gestured toward someplace behind Tess "—Dr. Redigo is one-eighth Osage. Join us won't you, Cord?"

Tess's jaws locked. Was he still there? She heard the tap of his boot heels on the bricks as he approached. Quillan was chuckling. "Why, between the three of us, I'll wager we could take this inn away from you palefaces, Jewel."

"Palefaces?" She giggled like a schoolgirl. "I'm afraid I wouldn't know a pale face from a pumpkin pie." She tugged her hand from Tess's and wrapped her shawl more securely about her shoulders.

"Are you chilled, Jewel?" Quillan asked softly.

"Perhaps, a little." She smiled in his direction. "I could ask Sugar to brew up some tea, if you would read some of your poems to me in the morning room.

Very few guests go there, except to get a book from time to time."

"Wonderful. I'll settle you in, and dash to get my portfolio." He turned to Tess and Cord. "If you two will excuse us?"

"Of course," Tess offered with a smile. She liked Quillan. It was evident that her aunt and the professor had become fast friends very quickly. She had a thought. "Oh, Quillan? Where is your granddaughter?"

"Asleep. She and I have drawn the 6:00 to 10:00 a.m. shore surveillance watch."

Jewel gasped. "Oh, heavens, then you need to get to sleep, too, Quillan."

He laughed, patting her hand. "Never mind me. I thrive on very little rest." Coaxing her forward, he added, "Especially when in the company of a lovely woman."

They'd disappeared inside before Cord said, "Good-looking couple."

She faced him, finally. "For once, we agree on something."

His expression grew somber, somehow sad. "Look, Tess, I've been wanting to—"

"Hey, you two, I've got the table set up and the coffee's ready." Nolan waved from the door. "Let's get started. Fred's shuffling."

Cord's eyes had been so luminous, so sincere as they'd held her gaze, but when Nolan called them, he looked up, breaking the spell. Tess felt like a string had been cut, and had the oddest sensation of stumbling, but she hadn't moved a muscle. She wanted to curse.

What had Cord been going to say to her that had made him look so seductive...no! She grimaced. Not that. At least she didn't believe his look had been knowingly sensuous. His eyes had been earnest, fervent. Full of emotion.

Something had happened between them—for one split second—something very close to what she'd wanted to happen thirteen years ago. Or had it? Was it just the play of light that filtered out from behind lace curtains?

"Coming," Cord called, sounding strained. With a hand at her elbow, he maneuvered her toward the inn.

"What were you going to say?" she whispered.

"Not now," he murmured under his breath. "Look, I don't want to cause any more hard feelings between us. Are you going to hate me if I beat you at bridge, or would it help if I let you win?"

"Let me win? You and who else?" Old irritation surged up her spine.

"Fred."

"I've never come up against such a colossal ego!" she spat out, never raising her voice, but each word quivered with tension.

"There's not much night life on Grande Comore. I'm damned good at bridge." He'd said it matter-of-factly, without pride or affectation. "I just thought you—"

She laughed shortly and without humor. "Modesty just might become you, Doctor. Why don't you try it sometime?" Hurrying ahead of him, she took Nolan's hand. "Let's go. I feel my second wind coming on."

Nolan grinned. "That's my girl."

"Cord thinks he's going to beat us," she remarked loud enough for her tormentor to catch.

Nolan snickered. "Oh, he does, does he? Well, we'll show him a trick or two." He put his arm across Tess's shoulders and led her toward the drawing room. Though Tess had won a verbal round with Cord, in the pit of her stomach, she didn't feel particularly triumphant about it.

AFTER TWO HARRIED DAYS entertaining Nolan, Tess once again busied herself with concerns of the inn. She took her aunt's breakfast tray out to her and chatted a few minutes with Jewel, Quillan and his eleven-year-old granddaughter, Natalie Quimby-Park. Once back in the kitchen, she settled into a straight-backed chair at the long kitchen table and tried to concentrate on writing the week's menus.

Out of the corner of her eye, she could see Sugar gyrating near the sink, earphones in place, and peeling apples for pies. Every so often she bellowed an off-key "Yah-yah-yah—whoooooooooo!" which wrecked Tess's already marred concentration, but had no effect whatsoever on Virge, who was in his corner chair, sound asleep.

Tess flipped a page in her notebook, her mind only half on her work. The other half was trudging along a well-rutted path that led to Cord Redigo. He and Fred Summerfield had trounced them at bridge the other night. Cord had been painfully patronizing, suggesting the cards had just fallen his way. She made a face. Sure, like Niagara Falls was just a slow leak!

He was good. She had to admit it, if only to herself. Two grand slams? He was more than good. He was damned good.

The rest of the weekend, even though Nolan had kept her busy, she'd seen enough of Cord to keep her emotions tied up in knots. Continually thwarted by her faltering ability to ignore this man who so badly needed ignoring, she jerked a hand through her hair for lack of a better outlet—such as drawing and quartering a certain cocky marine biologist.

"Mornin'," Cord called as he bounded down the steps two at a time. "Coffee smells good."

She closed her eyes and drew a calming breath before facing him. "Help yourself," she offered as blandly as she could.

"You?" he asked as he drew a mug from the shelf.

She met his gaze. It was warm, questioning. She stifled an urge to be affected by it. Shrugging, she feigned disinterest. "Sure."

She hadn't figured into her blasé response that he'd have to bring the cup to her; that she'd have to smell the pleasant, early morning richness of his cologne, or have a front row seat for his crooked grin.

"What are you doing?" he asked casually, turning a chair around backward and swinging a leg over the seat to straddle it. When he'd settled down, his thigh brushed hers.

She shifted in her seat, separating them a fraction. "Working on this week's menus."

He peered down at the page she was working on. "What's this?" A long, tanned finger pointed out one item.

"Baked halibut," she deciphered.

He raised a brow. "That's what I thought."

"What's wrong with it?"

He smiled at her, making her stomach flutter. "I have some very close friends who are halibut."

She almost smiled in spite of herself. "I've heard that halibut are not very discriminating fish."

He gave her that half smile that heated her dreams, and took a sip of his coffee.

Avoiding blue eyes that taunted and teased, she made a show of writing "Dr. Redigo: Peanut butter sandwich."

"Grape jelly," he suggested easily.

Not looking up, she scribbled the addition. "We don't usually cater to our guests this way."

His chuckle drew her gaze. "You're too good to me, Miss Mankiller."

She swallowed at the warm, honeyed feeling in her chest that his soft laughter evoked.

Virge's loud snore drew their attention. Tess put down her pen and sighed heavily, looking at the inert form in the corner.

"What exactly is his job here?" Cord asked.

"Janitor." She shook her head. "I envy Virge. He's such a lazy slob, and yet he's still so well loved—" She wondered what had possessed her to say that. And to Cord of all people. Wishing she could bite off her tongue, she cast him a surreptitious glance. His expression had become quizzical, but he said nothing. Plucking up her pen, she flipped a page, muttering, "I need a cigarette."

Movement at her side surprised her. Did Cord have cigarettes? She thought he'd said he didn't smoke.

"Here," he said, handing her a stick of bubble gum. "Sometime when you have a few minutes, read what the surgeon general has to say about smoking."

She looked up and caught her breath. His smile was rich, delicious. Her dazed reaction made her angry—more at herself than him. Still her anger, sensible or not, made her want to slap the grin right off his face. But Sugar would surely notice and then nag her endlessly to get at all the sordid details. Nothing was worth that kind of interrogation.

Collecting herself, she tossed her hair over her shoulder. "What exactly is your mission on this planet, Doctor? To follow me around and make me crazy?" She snatched the gum and fumbled with the wrapper.

He brought his coffee mug up to his lips and blew softly into it, his eyes searching hers across the rim. "Do I do that?"

His soft gaze stirred her and she squirmed a little. "Only in the *least* complimentary sense of the word." Wanting to do something to offset his unsettling look, she shredded the paper from the gum and tossed the stick in her mouth, chewing furiously. "Well," she fairly shrieked, though she was trying to keep her voice low, "Don't you have a snappy comeback?"

"Nothing comes to mind," he said with a note of seriousness that portended intimacy. "How about a boat ride?"

"A what?" She was taken off guard by his change of subject and the odd tone in his voice. A boat ride—

alone with Cord Redigo? "Not a chance," she told him in no uncertain terms. "You forget, we're not exactly chums."

He lifted a brow, but his smile didn't waver. Apparently he'd anticipated her rejection. "Maybe we can change that." He took her hand, jarring her, and went on, "I need to move some infrared camera equipment out to an island. Everybody on the team is either asleep or on watch." Standing, he tugged on her fingers in mute appeal.

"I—I don't go out on the lake much," she stammered, thrashing around for an excuse as she felt herself weaken. "I almost drowned once . . . when I was five . . . in a lake. . . ."

"Fate's interesting." His grin was artless, endearing. "I grew up in the middle of the country and became a marine biologist. You're afraid of lakes and you live on one."

She didn't know how it happened, but she was standing now, her fingers entwined with his as he gently coaxed, "What do you say?"

She knew she would go. There was just enough of that sixteen-year-old fool inside her to keep her from being intelligent about this. Her gaze dropped to his hand, holding hers. "Well, for Champ's sake . . ." She sighed, feeling bitterly betrayed by her own good sense. "I guess I could help."

"Thanks." He squeezed her hand.

She avoided his eyes, wishing her pulse would quit racing.

4

CORD WHEELED the powerful cabin cruiser around a point of land. The maneuver nearly sent Tess sliding across the bench seat into his arms. She grabbed the metal awning support and prevented an embarrassing tumble.

"The sheriff's office in Vergennes notified me early this morning of a Champ sighting in the area," Cord shouted over the wind and the hum of the cruiser's motor. "Since we don't have enough people for visual surveillance this far down the coast, cameras equipped to take time-lapse pictures with both regular and infrared film will help us view the surface of the lake. We'll get several hundred shots per roll."

Tess held on to the metal bar with one hand and swept her hair from her face with the other. They were high up on the flying bridge where wind swirled and whipped around them. "What's the infrared film for?" she shouted.

"Night surveillance." He pushed a lever forward and the boat began to slow, though Diamond Island was still only a dot on the horizon. Tess turned to look at him. "Why are you stopping way out here?"

"Sonar shows rocky shallows. Can't get much closer with the boat."

She turned to face him directly. "You can't get to the island?"

"I'll get there." He turned off the motor and smiled at her. "First, we drop anchor. Let's go down on deck." He preceded her down the ladder to the cockpit, and once she stood beside him on the teak deck, he said, "The inflatable rubber dingy will have to take over from here. Mind getting it out? It's in a compartment across from the helmsman's seat."

She cast him a doubtful look. "What does it look like?"

"It's that leather swivel chair over there with the wheel in front of—"

"I don't mean the helmsman's seat. I figured that part out." She frowned. Did he think she was a total idiot?

"Oh." He grinned, his eyes glinting with fun. He nodded toward a stowage compartment beneath the shelter top. "The inflatable dinghy's the only thing in that cabinet." Heading toward the bow, he added, "Except for a few CO_2 canisters."

She knelt and opened the compartment. "Inflatable rubber dinghy," she mumbled. The words didn't have the solid sound she preferred in a boat's name—such as battleship or supercarrier. Inflatable rubber dinghy sounded more like something a two-year-old would play with in his bath.

Well, there was one consolation, she decided. A boat that could be kept in a two-foot-by-two-foot space couldn't possibly carry more than one person. That was a break for her.

When Cord returned, she was lugging the heavy black bundle from its compartment. Before she had figured out how she was going to lift the ungainly thing, he took it from her, moved to the open stern and pulled a yellow tab. There was a loud hissing as it swelled and puffed and became a bulging black mass that looked more like an army surplus kiddie pool than a dependable means of transportation over water.

When the monster had given out its last angry hiss, she quipped, "Well, what'll they think of next—a floating ashtray?"

He smiled mildly and hoisted the thing over the brass railing of the boat. She watched, asking, "So this is an inflatable rubber dinghy?"

"Uh-huh." He eased it into the water, securing it with a nylon line.

"And you're going to take the cameras over to the island in this?"

He turned back to face her. "We are." He opened a hatch and hopped down out of sight before she registered what he'd said.

"What?" she belatedly shouted, dropping to her knees beside the hatch. Before she could insist that he was out of his mind, he was there before her, hoisting up two oars.

When he had jumped back out on deck and was towering over her, she demanded, "What do you mean, *we*? I hope you have a frog in your pocket, because I'm not going anywhere in that . . . that . . ." She faltered, pointing back toward the small craft being buffeted by the waves. "That oversize bathtub stopper!"

He didn't say anything but went forward, disappearing into the cabin. A moment later he returned, carrying two tripods and a large leather bag.

She clambered to her feet. "Did you hear me?" she asked, her chin stubbornly jutting.

"Yep." He was still smiling. "But you're going. The equipment's delicate and the water's rough. I need your help." Handing her one of the tripods, he reminded her, "Remember. It's for Champ."

"I—I said I'd help Champ. I didn't say I'd die for him."

Cord chuckled, walking past her toward the stern and the bobbing dinghy. "What if I told you I'd never lost a passenger."

Clutching the tripod nervously to her breasts, she caught up with him. "Oh, yes? Well, I bet the captain of the *Titanic* said something very similar about the time the iceberg was slicing his little floating city open like a can of tuna! And this . . . this—" she indicated the dinghy with a toss of her head, "—is no *Titanic*."

Cord quirked a brow. "Let's hope not." He leaned over the stern and deposited the oars in the bottom of the small craft. When he turned around, he took the tripod from her tense arms. At least he tried to. She was holding on to it for dear life. He looked into her stricken face, his easy grin fading. "Are you really that frightened?"

Yes, I'm frightened! she wanted to scream. *If you'd almost drowned when you were five years old, you'd be afraid, too!* But something in his eyes made her hesitate. Was it disappointment in *her* that she saw in those blue depths? Did he think her a coward? Did he pity her for her timidity? Pity! Well, he'd better not pity her! Nobody pitied Tessa Jane Mankiller!

"Frightened?" she echoed gravely, her chin taking on an imperious angle. "What is this, some kind of a schoolboy dare?"

"No, I—"

"Well, I'm not frightened. I'm just . . . cautious around deep water." She thrust the tripod into his arms. "Just tell me what needs to be done and I'll do it."

The tripod landing in his midsection elicited a barely audible "Whoof" from Cord. "Thanks," he returned a little hoarsely. His expression doubtful, he scanned her taut features. In response to his silent concern she averted her face.

After depositing the tripod in the dinghy, he turned back to her. She was standing rigidly, staring off into the distance. "Here . . ." he said and she felt his fingers close around her hand. She stiffened at the unexpected contact. "Let me help you into the boat, then I'll pass you the camera bag."

With high irritation and a heavy reluctance, she allowed him to assist her into the unsteady raft. Against her will, her body made careful note of every warm, lingering touch of his hands, first holding hers, then moving to her waist as she stepped into the sagging middle of the dinghy. Once she was seated, he handed her the camera bag with instructions to cradle it carefully in her lap.

The trip across the hundred yards of open water began in oppressive silence. But soon enough, Tess realized that there was something quite tranquil about watching the water trail by the boat, the frilly little swirls made by Cord's oars as he moved them quickly over the choppy lake, the lapping sound against the wet rubber.

It took her less time than she could have imagined to feel relaxed in this foreign element. Just as she was about to tell him so, Cord drew in his oars. She felt a thrill of anxiety. "What are you doing?" she asked, her voice taking on a forlorn note. She didn't like the idea of floating aimlessly with this man, or being in such close proximity with only a camera bag between them.

He passed her that crooked smile of his, but this time it didn't reach his eyes. "I apologize for this little deception. I didn't really need help, but I couldn't think of any other way to get you alone."

A shiver of trepidation rushed up her spine. "Alone?" she croaked. Clearing her throat, she asked, "Why?"

"Because of what happened between us thirteen years ago," he said quietly. "I want you to know how sorry I am. I was a thoughtless bastard, and I deserve everything you've said to me, every damning look...." He paused, his gaze skimming her wide-eyed face.

She tried but failed to discern any false inflection in his tone. His voice was deep, his expression serious. She felt so flustered, so shocked by his sudden confession that she didn't know how to react to it. Chewing the inside of her lip, she feigned interest in the distant Adirondacks. But for once, their spectacular beauty didn't stir her. She was too confused, too upset.

"I was hoping you could forgive me. I swear, if you'd been my sister and some guy had done to you what I did, I'd have killed the bum with my own hands." His voice had grown so harsh that she couldn't keep her eyes averted any longer. When she looked at him, he was watching her with a compelling intensity. There was real pain in his eyes.

The look unsettled her. Unsure of herself, she adopted a mask of indifference, which she was far from feeling. "I didn't have a brother," she reminded him flatly.

"I guess I should be grateful you didn't."

At her continued silence, he turned away, a look of self-disgust etched on his face. She examined his profile, alert and watchful for any sign of deception or manipulation. He looked nothing if not miserable, and she was touched by this glimpse of his vulnerability. He, too, had suffered. Learning that came as a shock, but it was also a healing revelation.

She'd hated this man for thirteen years. Hating him had done her no good—bequeathed her nothing but more sadness, more anger. Maybe it was time to make amends. To lay to rest something that, to be brutally honest, had been more her doing than his.

Cord's profile was rawboned and strong, his lashes long, light brown and tipped in silver. But lines of strain showed at the corners of his eyes. His aquiline nose flared, and his jaw bunched and flexed in his agitation. The handsome, crooked smile was gone, his mouth now narrowed into a tight dash. His distress grew hard for her to bear.

When at last she made her decision to offer a truce, she felt not the slightest bit begrudging. "I—I forgive you, Cord." The words were almost a sigh. "And, in all honesty, it wasn't entirely your fault. If I hadn't gone out there . . ." She couldn't go on. Instead she finished in a whisper. "I'm sorry, too."

She wasn't sure her words had reached him at first. But after a brief pause, he turned to look at her, his broad shoulders relaxing slightly. His eyes glistened with tears of gratitude.

She grew very still, hardly breathing. The early morning sun shone golden on his broad shoulders and made a halo of his blond hair, giving him an ethereal beauty. Though his gaze rested gently on her face, there was something erotic about his look that stirred her against her will.

He didn't reply immediately. When he did, he managed the barest trace of a smile. "Thank you, Tessa Jane."

The warmth created by those four words rushed through her, and she smiled back at him. It was a small, shy smile, but it was a beginning.

In the companionable silence that followed, he took up the oars and they resumed their journey. All too soon the ride ended with Cord jumping out in knee-deep water and hauling the boat up onto the rocky, barren shore.

Tess handed out the equipment, and then watched in silence as he set up the tripods and cameras and adjusted the timers. She studied him while he concentrated on determining the best angle for the cameras, checking delicate connections and securing the tripods against the gusty wind. She pursed her lips, thinking, once again, how knowledgeable and intelligent Cord was. At this moment it was hard to picture him as the egomaniac she had built him up to be. He was undeniably good-looking and wealthy, but he was also a highly respected scientist. It was no surprise that he was spoiled where women were concerned.

He walked a distance away from her and picked up a good-sized rock. His biceps bulged beneath his shirt, and she felt a tingle of feminine appreciation in the pit of her stomach. He deposited the rock against one leg of the tripod and stood, turning to face her at last. "That should keep it steady." He braced his hands on trim hips. "Ready to go back?"

His question pulled her from her unbidden thoughts. Just because she'd forgiven him didn't mean it was time to fall into the same old trap again! Abashed at her foolishness, she nodded, moving toward the small boat. She had only gone a few steps when Cord asked, "Are you going to marry him?"

The quiet question had the same effect on Tess as slamming headlong into an invisible wall. She stumbled to a halt. "What?" she asked incredulously.

"I said—"

"I know what you said." She pivoted to face him, feeling defensive. "My personal life is none of your business."

He wasn't smiling now. He met her troubled stare and held it. "You introduced Nolan as a good friend, but I got the feeling he'd like you to be more than that."

She threw him her most pointed you-must-be-crazy look. "I'm not discussing this with you."

He shrugged. "I didn't want a discussion. A yes or no will do."

"Oh, it will? Well, let me tell you . . ." She opened her mouth to say, in no uncertain terms, just exactly how much she didn't care what he thought would do, but the cutting words didn't come. Hadn't she just decided to try to be on more friendly terms with him? He stood there watching her, his expression solemn, questioning. What good would arguing the point do? Why not just tell him and get on with her life?

She let out a defeated sigh. "Why I'm telling you my private business is beyond me, but yes, I'll probably marry him as soon as the inn is solid enough to hire a manager." Actually, the inn was starting to run in the black, but Tess was still using that excuse to put Nolan off. She hadn't been able to explain the why of it to herself. "So now that that's cleared up . . ." She cocked her head in question. "Are you planning to commit matrimony with any of those halibut you know so intimately?"

"Isn't that question a little personal?" he asked without skipping a beat.

She groaned theatrically and turned away, stalking toward the boat.

He caught up. "Lost Cove Inn looks like it's in pretty good shape to me."

Tess pointedly ignored his remark, but she fretted that he might be able to read thoughts, since that same thing had just run through her mind. When she made no comment, he went on, "Surely Nolan, a CPA, would confirm that the inn is in solid enough shape so that you could marry him."

She felt a surge of anger at Cord's casual implication that she could marry Nolan immediately as far as *he* was concerned. She spun back to face him, snapping, "Any marriage proposals I've received are none of your business. Just because you made lo—" She swallowed, too embarrassed to say the word. Amending, she hurried on, "Just because something happened between us thirteen years ago, doesn't mean you have a right to butt into my private affairs!"

Her anger had inexplicably drawn her toward him, and they were now standing much too close. His breath was warm against her forehead, as he said, "Then he's asked you, and you've put him off. Why?"

"I just told you," she shot back, her voice shrill.

A small smile crooked the corners of his lips. "I don't understand why the question makes you angry. Most women would flaunt marriage proposals in other men's faces."

"I don't happen to be most women."

"That's true. . . ." he murmured, slipping his arms around her and drawing her against him. Even as he did so, his eyes telegraphed the intimate message that she was about to be kissed. Her mind refused to compute it. The idea of being kissed by Cord Redigo was counter to anything she wanted to happen in her life. . . .

His lips brushed hers once, twice, taunting her mouth to open of its own accord to meet the firm warmth of his. Tess's gaze was wide in horror as she watched his lids close, and his long lashes come to rest against the tanned skin of his roguish face. The vision fluttered before her for an instant and then disappeared as her eyes, too, succumbed to the seduction his mouth and hands were weaving about her.

His scent, subtle yet wildly male, invaded her senses, stirring her out of her initial shock and fear, and reviving within her a long-buried need. She inhaled the rugged maleness of him and grew dizzy, the world tilting on its axis. Time and space eroded and crumbled about her. Her fingers, pressing defensively against his chest, curled around the cotton knit fabric, clutching, grabbing for balance, and she moaned against him, whimpering some mindless endearment that she knew she'd hate herself later for uttering.

He lifted his mouth a shade, nipping, teasing her lower lip as he murmured, "Why aren't you sleeping with Nolan?"

He claimed her mouth fully again. This time it was his groan that met her ears as he pressed her more intimately against him. His tongue darted into her mouth, thrilling her and making her body grow weak and pliant to his will. But her mind began to burn with the implication of his question.

Why wasn't she sleeping with Nolan? Why indeed? Just because Cord had made love to her once, did he think that she spent her nights having casual sex with any number of men?

His tongue was trailing along the inside of her upper lip. His hands were lost in the tangle of her hair, stroking lovingly. Pressed tightly against him, she could feel his growing desire, and even as her rage at his crude remark grew, something deep inside her cried out to leave it be—to let the kiss deepen, the passion grow. Even as she shoved him away and felt the sting of her own slap on her palm, her insides throbbed for more of him.

Her rage came out in a low, feline growl as she stumbled backward, her anger taking full control once she had gained enough space to regroup her flagging senses.

Bringing herself up with a quick, sharp oath she blurted, "My sex life is none of your business, Dr. Redigo!"

"You made it my business once," he reminded her, his voice vaguely husky.

She let out a shuddering breath, her whole body quivering in her effort to reign in her bitter resentment. "I assure you, I won't make *that* mistake again. I'm not nearly so naive as I once was." She stalked back to the rubber dinghy before spinning around and shouting, "Nolan is a solid, wonderful man, and I'll marry him when the time is right! Is that perfectly clear?"

The question required no answer. He gave none. He just stood where she had left him, rubbing his tingling jaw, his expression more curious than troubled. He looked lean and unrepentant, legs braced wide, silver-gold curls dancing across his tanned forehead.

Narrowed azure eyes held her captive, making her forget to breathe. Tess felt weak, horrified that her reaction to his kiss still raged through her body and she fought back tears brought on by an aching want.

THAT AFTERNOON after all the inn's daily crises seemed to be taken care of, Tess retreated to her basement workshop where she took up her latest kite, a newer, larger version of Champ. She thoroughly enjoyed her hobby of kite making. It allowed her time to be alone, to be quiet and escape from the incessant demands of people.

She pulled a piece of cane from the soaking bucket, preparing to glue and tie the wet strip to the backbone of her kite to form one of Champ's humps. She reached for the tube of glue, but decided to light up another cigarette first.

The incident on the island had kept rearing its ugly head all day, driving Tess to near distraction. Finally, an hour ago, she'd lost all of her hard-won resolve and bought a pack of cigarettes. She hated herself for her weakness, but...

She took a long drag, not feeling any better. Forcing herself to think of something other than Cord Redigo's mighty sexuality, she turned her thoughts toward Nolan Lamont. What a nice, solid man—a man of unimpeachable integrity, with a fine job, a lovely house. He'd always lived in Burlington, Vermont. Nolan wasn't a vagabond as her father had been, or for that matter, Cord Redigo, who spent half his life on the island of Grande Comore, and the other half in far-flung places such as London, West Berlin or San Francisco, giving lectures or doing research.

She winced and took another long drag. Her thoughts had pivoted in the middle of her why-I-should-love-Nolan-Lamont list and tugged her back to thoughts of Cord, *again*.

Juggling the cigarette, she unscrewed the glue and dabbed some on the cane, muttering, "Nolan doesn't *need* me for anything. I've spent my life being needed more than loved, and Nolan would love me for myself." She recapped the glue and inhaled deeply on her cigarette. Nolan loved her "spunk," as he called it. She quirked a humorless smile. She'd never really liked that word. Still, she decided a bit snidely, Nolan didn't nag her about her smoking.

She started to take another puff, but in a sudden rush of self-contempt, she stubbed it out with enough force to rattle the workbench and topple an empty soda-pop can. It clattered to the floor and rolled beneath the legs of her tall stool.

"Congratulations. I'm sure your lungs will thank you one day."

Immediately recognizing Cord's voice, she jerked around toward the basement entrance. What a bothersome nag he was! But an utterly handsome one, she admitted with regret.

He'd changed for dinner, and was wearing a lush, chamois cavalry shirt, lizard belt with a silver buckle, and form-fitting denims. He looked ruggedly sophisticated standing there. She bullied back an urge to ride off into the sunset with him.

Meeting his crooked grin with a petulant lift of her brows, she said, "Don't tell me, you've come up with a sonar device for locating women."

"No," he responded, ambling closer. "But the idea's worth pursuing."

His relaxed, fluid gait both attracted and infuriated her. She turned away, curved the strip of cane around and tied it down with fine string. He was very near now. She tried to ignore him and the beckoning scent of his after-shave, but halfway through binding the joint, her fingers began to trip over themselves. With an exhale that was almost a curse, she put down her kite frame. "Do you mind?"

"What are you doing?" he asked, picking up a small hacksaw and turning it in his hand.

"Minding my own business," she mumbled, snatching the saw from him. "Be careful with that. You drop it and you could cut off a body part that's very dear to me."

He eyed her with speculative humor. "I'm gratified by your concern."

His suggestive rejoinder took her so off guard that she choked back a reluctant sound of mirth in spite of herself, and ended up coughing into her hand to discreetly cover it up. "I meant my foot!" she said, when she was able.

"Oh?" The guileless look on his face was almost believable. "My mistake."

Her lips twitched. He was incorrigible! Turning away from him, she entreated, "Will you go away?"

He had the audacity to remain where he was instead of turning on his heel and leaving as she'd asked. "I have some news I thought you'd be interested in."

"Oh? Don't tell me you've decided to reform and quit accosting innocent bystanders with your lips?" She didn't look up, but she could feel his gaze on her back during the oppressive pause that followed.

"I thought I apologized for that."

She peered over her shoulder at him. He had the grace to look a little ill at ease. She decided the best course would be to forget the whole painful incident. With a shrug, she asked, "Is the news about Champ?"

"It's about unexplainable readings on my paper chart recorder."

"Unexplainable readings?" She passed him a suspicious look before turning away to tie off the cane. "I suppose that's as good a way as any to belittle hard evidence."

"Erratic readings alone don't confirm Champ's existence. Still, they're not readily explainable."

"So *you* say."

She cut another strip of cane and put it in the soaking bucket, not because she was going to use it—she just didn't want to have to look up into those dusky blue eyes. "I'm not surprised about your so-called erratic readings. You'll eat your doubting words about Champ yet."

"You make cutting that cane look easy."

Easy? She'd never felt so clumsy in her life. Positive that she would slice off a finger if she tried it again, she put down her fretsaw and swiveled on her stool to face him. She was provoked but unsure exactly why. Cord had only come down here to give her good news. "Don't you have anywhere to go?" she asked rather grimly.

"Not until dinner." He peered at her thoughtfully. "Do you want me to go?"

"Yes, I do." It was only half true. Or maybe it was a complete lie. She was so confused!

He nodded, accepting her frankness with a resigned quirk of his brow. "If that's how you want it." He turned to leave.

"Wait!" she called, her need to have him out of her life warring with an insidious desire to have him near.

When he turned back around, she didn't know what in the world she was going to say. After a panic-stricken pause, she whispered, "Old habits die hard, Cord. Give me some time. I'll try to remember that we're . . . working at being . . ."

"Friends?" he suggested.

They looked at each other, in tension for a time, and then the tension passed. She lifted her hands in a kind of shrug. "I guess."

His smile was small, his eyes wooing. "Thanks." He motioned toward the wall where she had her colorful kites displayed. "Some of these are works of art. Do you ever sell them?"

Grateful to have something else to talk about, she said, "Sometimes I sell a few at craft shows. Mostly, I just love flying them. They're so free."

"What do you want to be free of?"

She'd been scanning her silken kites, her mind not really on them. When she heard his question, she darted him a startled look. "What do I want to be free of? Why, nothing! I—I don't . . ." she began, but her retort faded away, and she frowned. She hardly ever allowed herself to think about it, but she did want to be free of something. Only, why did it have to be just now that she'd had to blurt it out?

He was watching her quietly. "What is it?" he asked her after the silence had stretched too long.

She studied her fingernails. "You realize this is none of your business."

"I thought we were going to be friends. I'm a good listener."

Her gaze wandered restlessly from her hands to her lap. She realized with distress that her skirt had crept up along her leg under the workbench, and now a good portion of bare thigh was exposed to his view. She hurriedly tugged at her hem. And then her gaze fell on his chestnut boots, inches from the base of her stool; she followed them up to jeans that accentuated the muscled strength of his thighs, hips and— She averted her eyes, feeling an unbidden warmth flutter to life within her. "I, er, what were we talking about?"

"Freedom."

"Oh." His stance was relaxed, companionable. He had a way about him that invited confidences. She wished he didn't. It had been one of the traits that had made him so popular in high school. The pull of it was no less powerful now.

Even as a cautious part of her brain was demanding that she dash hell-bent out of the basement, she murmured, "I guess I want freedom from being needed all the time. My mother was sick, then my dad—he needed me. Aunt Jewel—I guess I'd like to be loved for myself alone—with all my flaws. Like Virge. No strings attached." She cringed, feeling like a total fool once the words were out of her mouth. To save face, she covered her embarrassment with a sharp little laugh. "Fortunately, Nolan loves me with no strings attached." She cocked her head defiantly before she added, "And *he* doesn't bug me about my smoking, either."

Some dark emotion skidded across Cord's face, making a tremor of apprehension skip up her spine. "What are you thinking?" she demanded.

He shrugged and looked away. "Nothing. It's none of my business."

She bristled. "I know it's none of your business. I told you it was none of your business." She lit a cigarette and blew a long, thin stream of smoke into the air before she could rein in her irritation enough to go on. "Now," she said, trying to control her quavering voice. "If you've got something to get off your chest, get it off."

He took the cigarette from her trembling fingers and stubbed it out, before asking her quietly, "You think Nolan doesn't need you?"

"I *know* so! What are you implying?"

"Nolan feeds on you, Tess," he began, his tone serious. "He needs wit and spontaneity in his life. Don't his visits drain you rather than revitalize you?"

She balked at the very idea, thinking his suggestion was utterly ridiculous. Wasn't it? It began to dawn on her that there was some small truth in what Cord said. Nolan's visits did drain her. He always insisted that she be "up," find things that they could do together, things that kept him entertained. Why hadn't she ever seen that as the neediness it was?

She tossed her hair back over her shoulder, trying to disguise her annoyance over the fact that Cord had seen something in two days that she hadn't discovered about Nolan in two years. Out of pure obstinacy, she shot back, "That's crazy, Cord. Go back to your precious fish. Maybe they'd appreciate your unsolicited opinions. I don't."

He might have winced, but she wasn't sure. Suddenly she felt disgusted with herself. It wasn't Cord's fault that she simply couldn't be objective where he was concerned. Still, that was no excuse for running roughshod over his feelings. She shook her head, muttering, "Now that was a lovely example of my wit and spontaneity."

He looked confused, charmingly so. Her smile was wan as she confessed, "That's my poor way of saying I'm sorry, Cord. You didn't deserve that." Wanting to make amends, as well as change the subject, she asked him, "Have you ever seen a monster fly?"

His grin was slow and somehow gallant. "Can't say I have."

"Then it's about time you did." Gazing into those soft blue eyes, she became strangely lighthearted. She hopped down from her stool and took hold of his fingers. The action surprised them both, and her eyes met his for a brief, startled moment before he turned her hand and took it in his.

"Are you telling me to go fly a kite, Tessa Jane?"

The soft way he said her name rekindled the yearning she'd felt when he'd kissed her that morning. She fought it, quipping, "How'd you guess?"

"No one's ever told me to go fly a kite before."

She averted her eyes. That didn't surprise her a bit.

5

THERE WAS JUST ENOUGH breeze for flying kites. High, delicate clouds like mares' tails were sketched on the cobalt sky. It was a beautiful summer evening, with at least an hour's light left. Tess became more at ease as she watched her silken Champ dip and sail and loft as Cord handled the reel.

"You're very good at flying kites," she said as she sat back in the cool grass, spreading her skirt around her. "Someone should have told you to do it long ago."

He laughed, letting out more line. "If anybody had told me a week ago that today I'd be flying a kite that's half snake and half whale, I'd have told them to seek professional help." He smiled down at her. "I presume this is your artistic conception of a zeuglodon?"

"Yes, it is. I copied it from a very scholarly library book." Feeling playful, she leaned back on her elbows, matching his grin. "From your tone, I presume you have a problem with it."

He looked away as the kite arced downward. "Just a suggestion. Most Champ enthusiasts prefer the plesiosaur as the monster of choice. I've got a picture of one if you'd like to see it."

"In your wallet, alongside your halibut buddies?" she teased.

"No, the coelacanths would be jealous." When he looked back down at her, his eyes were twinkling. "It's in a book about Champ. A friend of Mary's wrote it."

She arched her brows. "Do you mean to say you actually own a book about Champ?"

"Mary does. I've read it."

"And?" she prodded.

He turned his attention back to the kite, reeling it in a little. "And my choice would be the plesiosaur, too. You'd get more loft with added flippers."

She heaved a theatrical sigh at his sidestepping. "Dr. Redigo, you can be a real pain in the neck." There was a trace of laughter in her voice that she couldn't suppress.

"Mary's told me the same thing a time or two, but the anatomical location where I cause her pain is somewhat lower."

"Mary knows you better than I do."

His gaze dipped to meet hers. He said nothing, but she knew from his look that there were some things about him that Tess knew much better than Mary did. She swallowed and looked away. Movement out of the corner of her eye caught her attention.

Quillan Quimby was loping across the lawn toward them, waving broadly. He looked casually well dressed in gray whipcord slacks and a cream-colored cardigan sweater, a crest emblazoned on the left breast.

"Cord." Tess got to her feet. "I think Quillan has news."

Cord handed Tess the kite reel and walked toward Quillan, who was panting heavily by the time he reached the younger man.

"What is it, Quimby?" Cord asked.

"We've had word—" he put his hand to his chest, taking a deep breath "—from Basin Harbor about a sighting. Champ's heading this way!"

Quillan's face was flushed with a mixture of exertion and excitement as he went on, "And . . . just before the phone call, Jewel was saying she sensed Champ's presence." He clapped his hands. "This could be it, my boy. Should we gather the team and proceed to the boat?"

Cord pursed his lips and nodded. "Only shore surveillance people need stay on duty. The rest of us will do a visual tour of this section of the lake."

"Aye, aye, Cap'n," Quillan called over his shoulder as he dashed back along the lawn.

Cord turned to Tess, who was reeling in the kite as quickly as she could. "You heard?" he asked.

"Yes, and I hope you'll let me come."

Though his gaze was mild, there was an unmistakable sultriness hovering at the corners of his smile, as he offered, "Anytime."

She felt a stab of desire at the suggestiveness of his remark. Trying to keep the strain from her voice, she said, "I'll just put my kite away and meet you at the dock."

"Five minutes?"

"I'll be there."

He turned to go. Her gaze lingered, hungered for something she knew she shouldn't want. But a part of her sang with excitement at his veiled sexual invitation.

She was disgusted with herself. Her logical side argued that Cord probably hadn't meant anything sexual at all. On the other hand . . .

She clamped her jaws shut, fighting her wayward thoughts. If it *was* an invitation, Cord Redigo would make the same offer to any female with the breath of life in her. *She* certainly wasn't anything special to him!

Stalking off toward the inn to deposit her kite, she vowed to save her primitive urges for sweet, dependable Nolan. She tried not to think about the fact that she felt no such urges for him. An old fear began to gnaw at her. She so wanted to feel for Nolan the way she felt with Cord that night in the hay long ago. But she didn't. She sputtered an angry oath. More than anything in the world she wanted to quench that smoldering fire she harbored for Cord and be able to love Nolan the way he should be loved.

Fifteen minutes later they were cruising over rough water toward Basin Harbor. Mary was at the wheel on the flying deck, with Quillan, his granddaughter and Cord sharing the bench with her.

Most of the rest of the excited team had crowded onto the foredeck. Because Tess was so afraid of drowning, and because the foredeck had only the bow safety rail between life and nothingness, she opted to remain back in the deckhouse. Unfortunately, shortly after she'd made her cowardly decision, Cord bounded down the flying deck ladder to get some readings on the sonar chart recorder that was fitted into the hull beside the pilot's seat.

The wind had picked up, making the ride rough. Without warning, Tess found herself in Cord's arms as they lurched into the trough of a large wave. With a gasp she tried to twist away, but her balance was off and she merely succeeded in falling against him once more.

He grunted with the impact. "Well, hello," he murmured a little hoarsely.

She looked up at him with a mute, helpless regard. He flashed a grin of dazzling whiteness and drew her almost imperceptibly closer. "This is an unexpected pleasure."

She could think of nothing to say. For some reason her repertoire of snappy comebacks seemed dismally lacking.

His fingers were caressing her back, and his breath was warm on her face. The world around her shrank stealthily away. All she could see were his lips, so near, so tempting. All she could feel was his body, hard against hers, and the slow, rhythmic thudding of his heart. Reason deserted her and she could think of no rational reply—nothing but Kiss me, Cord, and that was far from rational! "I—the boat tilted..." she stammered.

"And you realized you hadn't hugged your marine biologist today." His voice was light, his eyes twinkling with mischief.

She frowned, muttering, "You think you're funny, I suppose."

"Why don't we talk about me later?" he whispered. "Right now we're being watched."

She stiffened in his arms and glanced over her shoulder. The elderly Inch sisters, twins, dressed identically in yellow cotton shirtwaists, were giggling and staring at them through the cockpit window.

"Oh, no . . ." she moaned.

A chuckle rumbled in his chest. "I knew you'd be pleased."

"Will you let me go?" she whispered curtly, her cheeks hot.

"Can you stand up by yourself?"

"I'll take a stab at it!" Pressing her hands against his chest, she berated him. "I would never have fallen if you'd given me some room. Can't you go to the back of the boat, or down in the basement or somewhere?"

His laughter was low and rich, drawing more gazes. "A boat doesn't have a basement, Miss Mankiller. In nautical terms, we call it the bilge."

"What do you call a knee in the groin—in nautical terms?"

His lips quirked with amusement. "I'd call that painful." For an instant it looked as if he just might kiss her. He didn't, and some irritating little part of her wasn't completely happy with his decision. As a matter of fact, she'd actually closed her eyes in anticipation—for the briefest instant—just as he'd let her go and stepped away. When she focused on his face again, his eyes were glinting devilishly.

Indicating the chart paper that was rolling out of the sonar recorder, he said, "Let me know if you see anything that looks like one of your monster kites on that." Before she had time to answer, he was swinging up the ladder to the flying bridge.

She slumped into the helmsman's chair and stared, unseeing, at the strip of paper as it slowly unrolled with its treasure of sonar information. She was too distressed to care what it revealed.

Dropping her head in her hands, she sighed loudly. She was cursed, that's what she was. Cursed with a rare sexual dyslexia where Cord Redigo was concerned, knotting up every physical encounter, saying all the wrong things. Then, incapacitated, she was forced to watch while he swaggered off, looking roguish and unbothered.

She scanned the faces of those on the bow. They'd turned away to scout for Champ again. She was grateful for that, at least, but her nerves hummed with dissatisfaction.

NOTHING OF CHAMP was sighted that day. In fact, nothing worth mentioning happened for the rest of the week. Tess kept as far away from Cord as she could. She grew short of breath and fidgety whenever cursed fate threw them together. Every time he ambled her way, she had the urge to run and find a necklace of garlic to ward off the spell he seemed bent on casting over her. In the presence of his easygoing cowboy quality, his unique elegance and ruthless sexuality she felt utterly bedeviled.

Oh, in court she'd have had to swear that Cord had been a perfect gentleman, and his conversation had been absolutely unblemished by overt suggestiveness. His eyes, however, had not been quite so pure.

They'd teased her, made promises to her, told her that in his arms, her body would writhe with ecstasy, that it was within his power to end the painful longing he knew was eating her up inside.

One such encounter, insidious in its apparent innocence, still bothered her. He'd stopped her as she headed out of a third-floor storage closet with several bars of soap for her aunt's apartment. He'd asked her for a bar, but the unspoken conversation between them had been pure sensual interplay. His eyes had probed the sexier precincts of her consciousness, telling her that he could take her and that bar of soap into their shower and lather up more than suds.

After handing him the soap and watching him walk away with a spicy John Wayne saunter, she'd careened off in another direction completely forgetting her original destination. She'd felt like a fool when she arrived at the front desk clutching five bars of soap to her chest. In a moment of true brilliance, she handed each of two departing guests a bar, explaining lamely that the miniature bath soaps were a traditional parting gift of the inn. Kalvin's gape-mouthed incredulity had been her just reward.

She'd begun to worry constantly. The invitation in Cord's gaze that day in the hallway remained quite vivid in her mind. But had it been real? Was she going crazy, or was he playing a very careful orchestrated game to wear down her defenses? If that was the case, then it was working. She wanted Cord Redigo to make love to her, and that scared her silly. Was she every bit as big a fool as she had been at sixteen?

To make matters worse, Nolan had come to visit on Friday evening. Several times Cord's remark about how Nolan "needed" Tess had come back to haunt her with something Nolan said or did. All too often, when it happened, her eyes had met Cord's knowing glance, and as the weekend progressed, she'd grown more and more infuriated.

A time or two, Cord had had the gall to egg Nolan on in his efforts to get Tess to entertain. This made her so angry that she could barely contain her fury, while Cord remained casually amused by it all. She wanted to slap him and kiss him at the same time. Her warring needs were tearing her apart.

Now it was Sunday afternoon and Tess was at her wits' end. Furious with Cord, she marched to his room to tell him in no uncertain terms how she felt about his interference. Seeing the door ajar, she barged in.

"Cord," she began, her voice controlled and low. "I need to talk to you, and I don't think you're going to like it."

"Fine." He nodded, but not in her direction. He was on the phone, his back to her. He looked tall, broad and casually chic in a dark-blue-and-red plaid shirt, buckskin pants and vest. She'd never seen buckskin pants before. She wondered how they felt—if they took on the hardness of his thighs and tight, rounded hips, or were they soft as velvet. . . .

"Thanks, I'll get right on it."

His words brought her back to why she was there, and she pulled her gaze away from his legs as he hung up. Without looking at her, he walked to the dresser and picked up a set of keys, but when he turned toward the door, he finally noticed her. The recognition in his grin was chillingly beautiful. "Hi, I didn't hear you knock."

She straightened her shoulders, feeling a little guilty. "I—I'm sorry, I guess I didn't. Your door was open. . . . I—I was thinking about what I have to say to you, Cord. We need to talk."

"Okay." He took her arm and led her toward the door. "But we'll have to do it on the move. There's a storm coming and I need to get the cameras off the island before they get battered to pieces."

"On the boat?" she asked, feeling a spasm of panic. "In a storm?"

"If we hurry, we can beat the storm."

"I don't like the 'if.'"

He chuckled but kept his pace rapid. She was dragged along, barely able to keep up with his lengthy strides. As they descended the steps to the dock, Tess squinted distastefully at the roughness of the water and the foreboding darkening of the sky.

The wind was racing around them in heavy gusts, swirling and tugging at her hair, tailored blouse and pleated skirt. She didn't want to go, but she knew that she had to get this said once and for all. If it took another boat ride to do it, then she would just have to deal with that, too. Besides, it looked as if Cord might really need help this time if his sensitive photographic equipment was to be salvaged.

THE WIND HAD PICKED UP while they were in the dinghy, and when they reached the island, the rain began. Cord ran for the cameras, shouting for Tess to secure the rubber boat, just as a powerful gust upended it. Though Tess held on to the rope, saving the boat from being swept away, one of the oars tumbled out and bobbed off out of sight.

Cord loped toward her, a large camera bag slung over one shoulder and two tripods jouncing on the other. He was squinting against the rain. Using both hands to cling to the boat's mooring rope, Tess could do nothing about the rain pelting her own face.

"Good work, saving the boat," Cord called over the wind and rain as he waded out and placed the camera bag and tripods in the bottom. "I'll help you in a second."

"We lost an oar," she shouted back, trying to shake wet hair from her face. "What'll we do?"

He waded back and lifted her into his arms. "We make do."

"There's really no need to carry me. I'm already wet," she told him irritably, noting all too clearly the solid warmth of his chest against her breasts.

"Your heels aren't very good for wading."

He was right about that. She said nothing. Shortly after Cord settled her in the boat, he pushed off and jumped in. Grabbing the oar, he began to paddle first on one side and then on the other in the direction of the cruiser.

The rain grew heavier, pounding them mercilessly while the wind chopped up the water. Tess was huddled in the bow, facing Cord. She turned to judge how far they had to go and gasped. The cruiser was lost behind a curtain of rain. Jerking around, she craned her neck past Cord. The island was also blotted out.

"Oh, my heavens, Cord. We're lost!" she cried, cowering back against the slippery rubber.

Cord continued to paddle, his expression closed and determined. His biceps bulged and bunched beneath his wet shirt as his efforts moved them forward. Or sideways. Or backward. It was impossible to tell which way they were going in the swirling maelstrom. "We're okay as long as we're afloat," he assured her, his voice betraying his struggle to keep the flimsy boat upright.

Tess looked down. The rainwater was collecting in the bottom of the dinghy. There was about an inch sloshing around. "Just how long do you think we'll stay afloat?" she called, her fear of drowning bringing her to the brink of hysteria.

The blinding rain turned suddenly to hail. Tess screamed when the first pea-size bullets of ice hit her. Cord drew in his oar and shouted, "Get to the middle of the dinghy!"

Too frightened to question him, she obeyed. As soon as she was settled there, Cord surprised her by pressing her backward. "Lie flat!" he shouted. "I'll cover you!"

"I'll drown."

"Rest your head on my arms. There's not that much water in here."

With his weight pressing her down, she could do little else. She could hear the hail pelting down all around her, making a deafening rat-a-tat on the dinghy. She wondered what sort of damage it was doing to Cord's back. She was still very aware of the stinging in her cheeks, shoulders and chest from the hail that had hit her before Cord had crawled over her. She hoped his vest would help protect him.

"How are you doing?" Cord asked her.

"I was just wondering the same thing about you. Does the hail hurt?"

He chuckled. She could feel it against her cheek. "Not as much as if we'd lost three thousand dollars worth of equipment. Thanks for your help."

"You're welcome." Rainwater, dripping off one of Cord's shirt buttons, wet her lower lip. She inhaled the clean scent of the storm mixed with the pungent soaked leather and Cord's musky warmth. After she'd taken a few deep breaths, her panic began to ebb. Even the water she was lying in didn't seem so cold anymore with Cord's arms around her, his legs sheltering hers.

His weight was not heavy on her. She realized he must be using a great deal of energy to hold himself up and keep from crushing her. Even so, she grew strongly aware of his vital body heating her through their soaked clothes. She had the unruly urge to take that dripping button in her teeth and rip it off, then run her tongue over the damp, furred hardness beneath the shirt, to make him groan with desire.

His muscled chest, warm through the wet clothes, tightened in his efforts to hold himself away, and she became aware of the heavy thudding of his heart. He made an odd noise in his throat and shifted as though to find a more comfortable position, accidentally brushing against her. She was shocked to feel him, bold and hard.

His muttered blasphemy was not lost on her as he shifted away. But he had not moved in time to quell the urgency his intimate touch had sparked to life in her. She tingled with a need to arch against him. Her sanity argued that initiating sex in an inflatable rubber dinghy awash with water and ready to capsize in a raging storm was madness, but her passion whispered slyly, *What better way to go?*

They were suddenly jolted with enough force to knock them both on their sides. Tess screamed and grabbed Cord's neck. "What—what was that?" she cried, terrified.

"I don't know." His voice seemed strained. "But at least it's stopped hailing."

"Good." She lifted her eyes to meet his. When their gazes brushed, something shockingly lusty passed between them. His face hovered closer, his eyes drawing her into a web of intimate meanings. Rain plastered their hair and their clothes, the wind blew cold and the lake bucked and kicked, bent on throwing them out. Still, she met his look boldly, accepting his overture, the right and wrong of it be damned. If she were going to die, she was going to do it with a smile on her face.

He read her desire and was lowering his lips to hers when they were jarred again by a blow to the side of the dinghy. This time, Tess clung to Cord's chest, hiding her face there. He drew her tightly to him, murmuring something unintelligible, but somehow comforting.

They were pushed along sideways by another bump, and then another. Tess lifted her head to look at Cord. "What's happening to us?"

He said nothing, just shook his head, but he seemed alert, concerned. "I think the rain's letting up." He raised himself on one elbow to look around.

Tess squinted into the drizzle, her eyes trained on Cord's face. She watched with surprise as his grim expression was altered by the familiar crooked grin. "Well, well," he said, pulling her up to sit beside him. "Look what we have here."

She leaned weakly against him, shivering from a combination of cold, passion and terror. Wiping water from her eyes, she looked in the direction he was pointing. To her amazement, the cruiser's stern was only a few feet away.

Grabbing the oar, Cord paddled the distance and helped Tess clamber onto the deck of the big boat. After offloading the camera bag and tripods he came on board and began securing the dinghy. "You go forward," he called to Tess, motioning toward the cabin door beneath the deckhouse. "There should be a couple of terry robes in the starboard locker beyond the galley."

She crossed her arms to stifle a shiver and stared blankly at him. "Where?"

He grinned as he slung the camera bag over his shoulder. "Go down the steps, past the living room and kitchen. There'll be a closet on your right."

"Oh." She nodded. "Where can I change?"

"Anywhere you want," he offered easily.

She raised a brow. "And where will you be?"

His expression grew serious and he looked quite endearing. His lashes were spangled with droplets of water, and rain was dripping off his chin. Quietly, he said, "Anywhere you want."

6

ENDEARING though Cord looked, Tess had regained her perspective and her sanity. She was no longer in the clutches of the Grim Reaper, so any rash plans she'd made while she'd thought she was dying were off.

Needing to avoid Cord's persuasive eyes, she bent and grabbed a handful of soggy pleats and wrung her skirt out on the deck. She did it once more on the other side before she looked back up. To be on the safe side, she pinned her gaze on his chin. "I—I won't be long." Without waiting for him to reply, she fled down the steps, past the tiny sitting room and kitchen and opened a narrow closet. There were two terry robes in it, both white.

With shaky fingers, she stripped out of her sodden clothes and donned the terry robe. Her hair hung wet and heavy down her back. Noticing a stack of fluffy white towels on a high shelf in the closet, she took one, wrapped her hair and coiled the whole bundle atop her head.

She looked around. There didn't seem to be any appropriate place to deposit her clothes, so she dumped them in the kitchen sink on her way back to the steps that led up to the cockpit. The carpeting felt good against her cold feet. She opened the door. "I've changed, Cord. You can come in."

He was hunched over the solar panel in the protection of the deckhouse. The rain was hammering down as hard as ever, but the buffeting was much less noticeable inside the cruiser. He looked up, first through the cockpit window and then down at her. His smile was wan. "I was hoping we could get back, but it looks like this storm is going to have its way for a while. I guess I'd better get out of these wet clothes."

She held the door open in mute invitation. "I'll wait out there."

"No need." He stood up and faced her. "I'll just use the forward berth."

As he skimmed past her in the narrow companionway, he stopped and smiled down at her. "You look nice in white, Tessa Jane."

Before she could absorb the quiet compliment, he'd turned away, calling over his shoulder, "I'll toss you a pair of socks."

"I—thanks," she said a little weakly, watching him eat up the small space with his long strides.

"When I get changed, I'll rig up a line to dry the clothes on." He pulled the locker doors closed between them. "We'll aim a couple of fans on them. It's the best we can do for now."

She nodded at nothing in particular.

"Have a seat," he called.

Dropping obediently onto a diminutive beige leather sofa that faced the companionway, she chewed on a fingernail. He thought she looked nice in white? She glanced down at herself and pulled the neck of the robe more closely around her. It was too big and tended to gape open. Good Lord, had it been gaping open when . . . ?

She closed her eyes and drew in a breath. Surely not. Working at getting her mind on something else, she looked around her. A fold-down shelf across from her held a compact stereo system and a small television set. There was a beige leather easy chair on her left and a small cocktail table, with a bowl of real fruit, directly in front of her. She debated between eating an apple or putting on some music.

Music won. She needed calming more than she needed nourishment. She got up and went to the stereo to browse through a stack of compact disks. She found one that suited her purpose and put it in the CD player. After a few seconds, the soulful voice of Smokey Robinson singing something about sleepless nights filled the cabin. The boat was rolling, but not alarmingly. Over the music, Tess could hear the rain. Or was it hailing again? Whichever, the storm outside had cast the cabin in semidarkness.

"You're a Smokey Robinson fan?"

"Yes. His music is quite restful."

He chuckled. "If you say so." There was a wicked note to his rejoinder that seemed to say he had put Smokey's music to more energetic uses.

She cringed, not wanting to think about it. Having no intention of pursuing that line of conversation, she changed the subject. "Mind if I turn on a light?"

Something plopped on the couch next to her, as Cord called, "For cold feet."

She eyed the balled tennis socks with suspicion. Exactly how had he meant that? She called back, "I presume that's a yes."

He laughed outright. "Turn on anything you want."

"Thanks..." She rolled her eyes heavenward. Either he was totally depraved or she was losing her mind, reading innuendos into his every word! "The light will do," she quipped, almost light-heartedly. Pulling on the socks, she curled her feet beneath her. A lamp attached to the wall flickered on at her touch.

"Better?"

"Cozy." She leaned her head back to rest it on the partition between the salon and the dinette. "It's like being rocked in a cradle."

"Sorry I can't offer you a roaring fire."

Her lips twitched into a reluctant smile. She felt oddly at home. "I don't think I could stand it," she murmured too softly to carry all the way back to him.

"I know what you mean," he remarked equally quietly, sounding so near that she jumped. "There's something special about being on a boat."

"Oh!" She touched her robe lapel nervously. "You didn't make a sound walking out here."

"It's the Indian in me. How about a little dinner?"

He was leaning on the bulkhead, grinning down at her, wearing the other white robe. His, however, was opened to the waist, showing a fetching expanse of bronze chest. A mat of golden hair caught and reflected the light from the lamp.

The robe was much shorter on him, exposing more than a hint of thigh. It should have been a capital crime to hide those legs, she mused. They were solid and gloriously male. Formidable quadriceps bulged above his knees, speaking of power and strength. His calves curled out wide and hard above well-shaped ankles. Tess had never thought of a man's ankles as sexy before. But looking at his, she couldn't fathom why not. She realized that he was talking and snapped her gaze back up to his face. "What?"

He took a step into the cramped little sitting room, which seemed even more cramped with his towering presence. "I asked what you'd like for dinner. It looks as though we'll be stuck here for a while."

A flash of lightning and an answering blast of thunder seemed to underscore his words. Wind battered hail against the hull of the boat as Smokey, in his dusky, jazz-clarinet voice began to urge someone to fulfill a need. She tried to brush aside the fact that the same idea had occurred to her the instant Cord had appeared in that white come-up-and-rip-this-off-me outfit. She nodded absently. "Yes—yes, food would be a good—" she had been about to say a good substitute; she decided against it; he would probably just ask a substitute for what "—would be good. Anything's good."

"I'm not sure my cooking deserves three 'goods,' but it'll be nourishing."

"While you do that, I'll hang the clothes."

"No thanks. Just relax." He flashed a splendid smile. "Let me *not* need you this afternoon, Tessa Jane."

There was something about the way he said her full name that made it sound like a caress. Trying to appear less touched than she was, she remarked, " 'Not need' me? That's very romantic."

"Do you want romance?"

"Don't be silly," she denied quickly. If she'd been the type to blush, she'd have been crimson. "It was a joke. What I meant was, I couldn't let you wait on me hand and foot."

"Force yourself." He surprised her by tracing a finger along her cheek. "Consider it my way of repaying you for getting you into all this."

The touch had been brief, but its effect was not. Her skin registered warmth long after he'd removed his hand to his robe pocket. She noticed that he balled his fist once the hand was out of sight. She wondered why.

Her gaze drifted to his face. His eyes were slightly narrowed, and his crooked mouth had lost much of its amused twist. She got the decided impression that he was suddenly irritated about something. "Dinner will be about fifteen minutes," he told her, turning away.

She was confused. Had she seen annoyance in his eyes? She wanted to know what was wrong. "Cord?"

He glanced back, waiting for her to go on.

She chickened out, deciding it would be safer to keep their relationship as superficial as possible. She improvised. "Do—do you have a brush I could borrow?"

"Sure." He indicated the door beside the companionway. "In the head."

"The head?"

That slow, beguiling grin was back when he said, "Take a guess."

TESS MOVED HER TRAY to the coffee table and stretched. "That was good, Cord. Thank you."

He was sitting in the chair that stood at an angle to the sofa. Lowering his coffee cup, he smiled over at her. "My mother always said nobody could open a can of stew like her baby boy."

Tess felt like giggling, but she restrained herself. "I can't picture you as anybody's baby boy."

He gave her a mock affronted look. "I'll have you know I was voted Broken Arrow's 'Baby Chubby Cheeks' when I was eight months old."

"Oh, really?" Unable to help herself, she asked, "Which set of cheeks made you famous?"

He chuckled and set his cup on the coffee table. "Let me put it this way. In the photo that won, I was face-down on a bearskin rug."

Laughter gurgled from Tess's throat. "I'd like to see that picture."

He sat back, stretching out his long legs between the coffee table and her sofa. Something in her stomach fluttered at the way the ripcord muscles flexed with the movement. His deep chuckle drew her attention. "You never will. I ate it when I was twelve."

"You what?" she asked, incredulous.

"My mother was about to show it to my best girl."

Tess couldn't hold back the laughter any longer, picturing this handsome, charismatic man, at the tender age of twelve, eating a photograph to save face. How absurdly sweet. She asked, "Did it surprise the girl?"

He looked a little sheepish. "It scared her to death. She grabbed the photo album she'd brought over and ran out of the house. I guess she thought I was going to eat her pictures, too."

"I gather the romance cooled."

"Like an Antarctic winter." His short laugh was almost wistful. "I was brokenhearted for a week."

"I'll bet. How was it?"

His expression grew curious. "The broken heart?"

She blanched, feeling a stab of old pain. She knew how a broken heart felt. Trying to hide her unease, she said, "No—the photograph."

"Oh." He shrugged. "Considering the alternative, it was ambrosia."

Lightning flashed, searing the room white, and a gust of wind riveted the hull with rain.

Being reminded of how much Cord's rejection thirteen years ago had hurt her had taken the fun out of their conversation. "Quite a storm," she murmured.

He'd grown serious, too, frowning slightly. "Yes. Strange."

"What do you mean?" She sat forward, alert. Was there danger she didn't know about?

He exhaled. "Nothing I can put my finger on. It was just that crazy jarring when we were in the dinghy. It seemed like we were being rammed by a log." He shrugged. "But there wasn't a log."

Tess uncoiled her feet, placing them on the floor very near his. "I'm no help. I've never been adrift in a dinghy."

He smiled without humor. "I try not to make a habit of it, either." He got up to remove their trays to the kitchen. "Want more coffee?"

"No thanks." Not satisfied to lay the subject aside, she followed him into the kitchen. "What, exactly, is bothering you about the jarring business?"

He set the trays down on the galley counter and turned to face her. "Nothing. It's just that we were very lucky out there. Almost too lucky."

She frowned up at him. "What do you mean, 'too lucky'?"

"Who knows?" He passed her a wry smile. "Maybe somebody down there likes you."

She blinked in surprise at his remark. "You mean Champ? Are you saying Champ saved us?"

He shook his head and chuckled. "Not a chance. It was probably just a freak combination of wave and wind action. Fortunately we were washed directly toward the boat."

"*Probably* waves and wind?" she repeated, her smile challenging.

His eyes took on a sparkle of amusement. "Be quiet, dreamer. Go in and watch an old movie or something. I have dishes to do."

"You're not still on that not-needing-me kick, are you?"

"Don't tell me you've had all the not needing you need."

She grinned in spite of herself. He exuded such a boyish charm. "You're crazy if you believe you can satisfy a lifetime of needing to be not needed in one afternoon. I just don't think you need to do all the not needing, that's all."

His grin grew bemused. "Say again?"

There wasn't much room between the counter and the dinette table. The rocking cruiser swayed them into thigh-to-thigh contact more than once. She was finding it hard to concentrate on any conversation, especially one that had taken such a nonsensical turn.

They brushed again. She wondered if he was feeling the same worrisome degree of discomfort as she.

He shifted, clearing his throat. "Go on. Get out of here."

She looked into his eyes, searching them in the dim light. Though he'd said he wanted her to go, she saw a completely different request in his gaze.

"Okay, I'll go. . . ." she murmured, and she meant to go, she really did. She didn't mean for her arms to move up and wrap themselves around his neck. She didn't mean to stretch up on tiptoe and tilt her head at just the right angle to be kissed. And she definitely had no plans for her lips to move in a husky, taunting whisper, "Am I gone yet?"

She pressed against him and saw the barest widening of his eyes. He was surprised—not shocked but taken off guard. Unsure what to do next, she could only smile tentatively, in wordless invitation.

For what seemed a long time he stared at her, looking as though he were battling some private war. At last he asked, "Are you sure about this?"

"Very sure." Her voice was breathy. "I'm a big girl now. Or haven't you noticed?"

"Hellfire, woman," he muttered. "I've done damn little else. . . ." Hauling her into a hard embrace he buried his face in her hair, kissing the softness, his hands moving, searching, arousing. "Tessa Jane . . ."

He lowered his mouth to hers, fulfilling every fantasy about how a kiss should feel, should taste.

She reveled in the glory of it, her tongue dancing and thrusting with his until their breathing became ragged with desire. Just when she thought she could no longer stand, she felt herself being lifted into his arms.

"I'm going to make love to you," he told her softly.

"I know. But I had to throw myself at you again." She smiled, nuzzling his chest, licking and nipping. For some absurd reason she had to ask, "Does this playing-hard-to-get ploy work every time?"

He kissed her forehead. "I was just about to ask you the same question." He carried her to the forward cabin, lowered her to sit on the vee berth and knelt before her. Looking up into her eyes, he undid the sash of her robe, parting the fabric until he could enjoy the sight of her naked beauty.

He slid his hands around her waist, making her gasp with delight as he leaned forward to kiss and nibble her belly. The slight roughness of his stubbled jaw sent a thrill through her, and she cradled his head within her arms.

His kisses moved down, and Tess closed her eyes in shuddering victory as he found her damp, restive core. She whimpered his name as he began to flick his tongue over her, suddenly frightened at the degree of intimacy he had so quickly led her to.

His response was reassuring and typically male; there was no retreat. He slid his hands down her back and cupped her buttocks, pulling her even more deliciously close. He kissed and sucked and pleased her so well that she could do little more than lie back and accept his gift as it was offered—hot yet unhurried.

She curled her hands in the sheets as divine tension built in her like flood waters behind a weakening dam. At last, with a kiss so deeply intimate that her body could no longer deny her ultimate gratification, Cord brought her over the brink to the most delectable sensations she had ever experienced. Surge after surge of voluptuous pleasure washed through her body, her whole being quaking with ecstasy.

A sob escaped her throat. She had never been given such a selfless, beautiful gift as this. Cord's first thought, his first passionate act had been to please her. How many times in her life had anyone cared even half as much about making her happy?

He had eased up beside her and was nipping at her shoulder where the robe had fallen away. She stroked his cheek gently, offering in a weak voice, "You didn't have to do that."

He paused for a second, then planted a very definite kiss on the tender skin of her throat before looking into her eyes. He sobered when he saw her tears. "Tessa Jane," he murmured, pulling her to him, her breasts molded lovingly against his chest. "You give so damned much. You've got to learn to take."

He kissed each tear-stained cheek, whispering, "I won't be long." He rolled away and in a few strides had disappeared into the head. After a minute, when her mind became somewhat less muddled, she realized he'd gone to put on protection. She'd been in such a wild state of passion, she'd forgotten all about taking precautions.

Turning on her side, she closed her eyes. Thunder exploded above her and rain pelted the hull. A faint smile curved her lips. Never in her life had she known such pure happiness. Cord Redigo might be very wrong for her in the long run, but in a few moments he would be back to wrap her in his arms, to thrill her as most women only dream of being thrilled. Perhaps later she would feel differently about all this, but right now she had no desire to be anywhere else on earth.

She heard a movement and opened her eyes to see Cord heading toward her, boldly, divinely naked. His blond hair was passion-tossed, his eyes glistening with soft promises. Her gaze moved to that part of him that was erect, primed for her and a shiver of giddy anticipation ran the entire length of her body.

When he was again beside her, taking her into his arms, she sighed languidly, feeling no regrets.

He caressed her back and then the rounded softness of her buttocks, turning her to look in his eyes. Very tenderly, he whispered, "You're a lovely woman, Tessa Jane." He kissed the tip of her nose. "I was in a lot of pain when I thought you hated me."

She smiled wanly, taking his face in her hands. "So was I, Cord." Sliding her arms around his neck, she lifted taut nipples toward his chest, teasing his flesh. "Now I see I never hated you. I was just afraid of being hurt again."

He groaned and pulled her to him, his lips brushing hers as he whispered, "I don't want to hurt you. I never did."

"I know."

They kissed deeply. She drew closer, wanting to know every inch of his body against hers.

Sensing her growing urgency, Cord pressed her hips to his groin. The hard length of him against her made her damp with hunger, and she moaned against his lips.

Sliding a hand down the back of her leg, he gently lifted her knee over his hip, adjusting himself against her. Shifting his hands to her bottom, he pressed against the place where she was most sensitive.

She sighed and pulled from his kiss to look into his eyes. They were closed, but as soon as she had drawn away, the long, light lashes flicked open. When he saw her looking at him, he smiled, and with a cunning move of his hips, made her gasp with delight again.

"What are you doing?" she asked, her voice weak with pleasure.

"Teaching you to take." Stroking her hip, he added softly, "Relax and enjoy the lesson."

With that, he thrust more deeply, but not completely into her. She moaned with the rush of erotic delight and closed her eyes. "Teach me," she pleaded softly.

At first his thrusts were slow, exotic torture, driving her almost mad with every exquisite plunge. Then, when her nails had begun to bite into his muscled back, he pressed her down on her back and blanketed her, becoming the carnal center of her universe.

Cord stole from her every vestige of timidity, and she took the pleasures he had to give with gusto. She cried out her delight, wrapping her legs about his hips to hold him prisoner within her. Joined as they were, she became a wild, free creature, at long last truly alive in his arms.

She could hardly believe that the mere biological act of mating could be carried to such dizzying heights. Cord lifted her to a sexual plane she'd never experienced before, a place both feral and frenzied. She loved, and was loved, in a reckless, heathen way. No longer the prim innkeeper in lace collars and pleated skirts, she had become a pagan temptress, a female animal stalking her prey and eating her fill.

Her body glowed with the joy of their exertion. When she had cried out her release for the third time, she lay back, exhausted, complete, full of Cord Redigo and full of the purest satisfaction imaginable as she felt him let himself go within her. Easing his body weight down, he held her close as he relished his own climax to the fullest.

His heart hammered against her breasts, and his breath was warm against her cheek. After a quieting moment, he teased the lobe of her ear with his teeth, half groaning, half sighing, "You're a witch, Tessa Jane. A sweet, shameless witch."

Lifting his head so that he could more easily see her face, he gave her a slow, careful scrutiny that made her feel devoured.

Her lips were numbed and well used, and her smile felt awkward when she tried it. Wrapping her words in a sigh, she told him, "You look like you want to eat me up."

He brushed aside love-tossed strands of hair from her rosy breasts so that his gaze could roam unhindered. "You read my mind."

She flushed at his deeply suggestive tone. "Oh, Cord . . ."

He grinned. "We have to pass the time some way. I'm no superman." He rolled off her, and she relished the quiver of heightened sensation even their parting caused.

She let her eyes drift over his lean nakedness. He reminded her of a sleek panther, and she felt new fire burst to life in her core. She was surprised at herself and she smiled, delighted with the Tess Mankiller that Cord's lovemaking had created.

"You don't give yourself enough credit," she murmured, following him over, her small, white teeth nipping his neck. With his half moan-half growl, she lifted her head, raking him with a mischievous look before pressing him back on the bed.

"Let's just time your recuperation, shall we?" She planted her hands on either side of his face, and then, with a womanly sureness of purpose, she lowered her breasts to his face. She closed her eyes as he began to tease, nuzzle and suck. Bringing his big, gentle hands up to cup them, he kneaded her flesh, drawing her all the way down so that he could bury his face in her pliant warmth.

She curled her arms about his head, kissing his musky hair. "How are you doing?" she queried, her voice low and breathy. "Need much more time?"

He groaned and nipped at her. He sounded so like a victim on the rack, she couldn't hold back a gurgle of laughter.

He drew his face away and looked up at her, his expression a quaint mixture of lust and confusion. "What's so funny?" he asked, his voice hoarse.

She sat back, straddling his belly, feeling quite powerful with her ability to bring this huge animal of a man to his knees with the merest twitch of her body. She grinned down at him. "I'd say it's been almost a minute. Don't you think?"

"Tessa Jane," he groaned, trailing a finger between the tempting mounds of her breasts. "Don't put a man in this condition and expect him to be able to think."

Impishly, she ran her nails down his chest, eliciting a low sigh from him. "A minute and a half, maybe?"

"I'm dying."

She cast a quick glance over her shoulder and then down at his expectant face. Grinning, she slithered backward toward her objective.

Her intimate, straddle-legged trip across his furred belly made Tess's body sizzle with need. More adeptly than she'd thought she could, she guided him home. When she had slid atop him, and fixed him hot and deep within her, she lay fully against him and whispered huskily, "Don't ever let me hear you say you're no superman, again . . ."

She both heard and felt his low chuckle. His hips lifted against her, drawing a flash of heavenly feeling. His arms came around her hips, pulling her lithe body to him once again, and with her gasp of rapture, time ceased to exist.

7

THE SKY HAD BEEN WASHED so clean by the storm that it sparkled. Inhaling the crisp, rain-washed air, Tess wondered why she'd never noticed that the heavens held so many stars before. She hugged herself. Her clothes were dry, but for a slight dampness in the waist and hem of her skirt. Cord had found one of Mary's old sweaters to drape over her shoulders. Still, the night's chill was beginning to set in.

"There are people on the dock," Cord called over the powerful rumble of the cruiser's engine.

His words hit her like a wet rag, pulling her back to a reality she would have preferred to avoid. She dropped her gaze to the lighted wooden platform jutting out from the shore. Sure enough, there was a small crowd hailing them. She saw Kalvin, most of the cryptozoologists and Nolan, waving broadly. Her jaw firmed with distress and she shot a pained gaze toward Cord. He was looking at her, his expression one of concern.

"You okay?" he asked softly.

She smiled with little enthusiasm. "Sure . . ." In his white twill pants, white cotton turtleneck shirt, tennis shoes and socks, Cord looked the perfect preppy sailor, his blond hair tossed in casual elegance by a capricious breeze. She felt limp and dowdy in comparison, and sighed.

"What's wrong?" he asked.

She shook her head. "I just wish you'd found those clothes of Mary's husband's before..." She looked away, unable to finish. She was timid and embarrassed about what had happened between them.

He touched her chin with long, warm fingers, forcing her to meet his gaze. "I don't think that's what you really wish, is it, Tessa Jane?"

He fixed her with an unwavering regard, waiting. She swallowed. "No, I guess—I wanted you—everything...but..." Her whispered words were laced with confusion and panic. What was she to do? After her reckless abandon in Cord's arms, how could she look Nolan in the face?

She avoided Cord's eyes, looking at his chest instead. He had a magnificent chest, she decided, then squelched the thought. "Cord," she began, her throat as dry as dust. "I want you to know that I don't regret what we did today. Really."

When he didn't speak, she made herself look into his eyes.

He felt a tug of regret. The lift of her chin, the sadness that glistened in the striking green depths of her eyes stirred him profoundly. Sensing her need, he helped her. "But you don't want it to happen again."

She nodded. "I—I guess there are just some people who are chemically attracted. Drawn together by nature rather than by true compatibility." She shifted her gaze and fastened it on the dock as they glided alongside it. "But besides that...unfortunate chemical thing, we really have nothing in common. Please . . ." She looked back up, her eyes pleading. "Since you have no intention of marrying me—" she held up a halting hand to ward off any objections, though he'd made no move to speak.

After an awkward silence, she added hastily, "Since we have no intention of marrying each other, I think we'd better keep our distance from now on. Will you promise to do that?" she asked, struggling with her overpowering feelings for him.

Something like distress flickered across his face before he averted his gaze and swung the wheel enough to ease them into docking position. After the maneuver was completed, he looked back at her, studying her face with narrowed eyes. When he spoke, his voice was low and rough. "I've been a lot of things, but, lady, I've never been a chemistry experiment." He lifted a skeptical brow. "Until you say different, I'll stay out of your . . . lab."

She could hardly believe her ears. What a raging egomaniac this man was! "I won't say different, Dr. Redigo!" she threw back. "Not until hell freezes over—twice!"

His head came up sharply, as though he'd been struck. After a few tense seconds, he said, "So be it." This time there was no trace of malice in his tone. He looked as if he had absolutely no problem with the idea, and that made her unaccountably sad.

Her vision became blurred with unshed tears. Why did she suddenly feel as if he'd just rejected *her?* What had she expected him to do—stomp around in a rage, arguing and sputtering oaths? She swallowed several times, trying to think of a stinging rejoinder, but nothing came, which was probably for the best. If she chanced speaking, she'd just humiliate herself by crying.

Cord turned off the ignition, and the world became deathly still.

"Ahoy, there!" Nolan's voice rang cheerfully across the air. "You two okay? We were worried, even though Cord radioed. You never know."

Nolan's lighthearted greeting hung in the air between them like a drawn sword.

Tension gripped tight in Tess's throat. She tried to swallow it and failed. Though she wanted to drag her gaze from his, she couldn't. When at last she found her voice, it was a reedy whisper. "We'd better go."

"Yes, ma'am," Cord agreed easily enough, but his expression was unreadable. "Wouldn't want to worry the boyfriend, now, would we?" He took her elbow and steered her toward the stern, giving her no opportunity to reply before helping her into Nolan's waiting arms.

Before Cord could hop down on the dock, Nolan had pulled Tess into a loving embrace and was kissing her tenderly. Cord busied himself securing the boat. Maybe it was true that he and Tess had nothing more between them than an unfortunate chemical thing, as she'd so analytically referred to it. But right now, Nolan was holding her in his arms, kissing those luscious lips, and it made Cord's skin crawl.

Before he could drive himself nuts about it, Mary was chattering away, dragging him along, telling him what had happened that day. A fisherman near Big

Snake Bay had thought he'd seen something "unearthly." He'd snapped several photographs, but it would be twenty-four hours before he could get the pictures. And just after the rain stopped . . .

Cord allowed her to tug him in her wake, but he'd long since quit listening. Apparently he was determined to punish himself for being so rash this afternoon, by keeping his eyes trained on Nolan. His arm was cinched greedily about Tess's waist as they walked up the steps toward the cliff. When Nolan bent to whisper some endearment in her ear, Cord felt a tightening in his gut and cursed.

"*What?*" Mary asked, shocked that out of nowhere her cousin had decided to singe the night air with blue language.

He found the grace to grin ruefully at the disgusted look on her face.

"Sorry." He searched for an explanation, but when nothing plausible came to mind, he offered vaguely, "I was thinking about something else."

She grunted. "Something charming, no doubt."

"Charming as hell," he mumbled.

"For an educated man, your vocabulary has a truncated feel to it tonight."

"My vocabulary isn't the only thing that feels truncated."

She gave him an odd look. "Well, we'll get back to that later. Right now, I'm curious about how you ended up taking Tess with you on your jaunt to the island."

"She came to my room. Wanted to talk. I was in a hurry, so I suggested we talk on the boat ride."

"What did she want?"

He pursed his lips in thought. "I don't know. We never got around to it."

She stopped in her tracks, dragging him to a halt beside her. Twisting to face him, she charged, "Cordell Merrett Redigo. You spent three hours out there alone with her in a storm-tossed cabin cruiser and you didn't get around to talking?" She planted her fists on her narrow hips. "Just how did you and Miss Mankiller pass the time? Or shouldn't I ask?"

He met her hard gaze and told her everything she had a right to know. "We got rained on saving the camera equipment you wanted me to save."

She tilted her head. It was an I-don't-believe-you gesture that he knew well. "Did you make a pass at that sweet child?"

"She's no child, Mary."

"Oh, Lord. That's the worst possible observation you could have made. You did make a pass, didn't you?"

He took her arm and began to tow her forward. "Would it matter what I said? You've made up your mind."

"You're damned right, I have," she agreed briskly. "I know how you operate. I still get letters from that underwater photographer who came on that Grand Cayman trip with us. Sylvia George. She says to tell you hi in every gooey letter."

"Tell her hi back."

"Not on your life. I'm not going to encourage her. You do enough of that all by your lonesome. Besides, I have a problem closer to home. Every time I go to the dentist, my hygienist, Beverly, keeps talking about your fantastic incisors."

"Beverly?"

"You know, Beverly Lane. Last summer you asked me to get you an appointment at my dentist? Beverly still talks about your teeth all the time, but I'm no idiot. That woman wants more of you than your bite-wing X ray."

"Oh, Beverly. Right." He recalled her now. Pretty blonde. "We had one date. All she took off in my presence was her jacket. I did nothing to the woman."

"*Nothing?* You bat those obscene lashes. You smile that deranged smile. I'll bet you plied Tess with wine out there in all that thunder and lightning and told her something about how great sex is on the stormy seas, didn't you?"

"We weren't at sea," he observed obliquely.

"Don't mince words with me. I was describing your seduction tactics. How close did I get?"

He shook his head at her, giving up. He might as well let her believe what she was going to believe anyway. "Amazing, Mary," he muttered. "It's almost like you were there."

She exhaled heavily. "Just tell me one thing. Am I too late? Did she resist you tooth and nail?"

"She used them with all her strength," he told her truthfully.

Mary smiled with relief. "Well, good. Still, there's no time to lose. I have a feeling she's attracted to you."

"Chemically speaking," he grumbled.

"What?" she asked.

"I was saying you ought to dump zoology and tell fortunes for a living. You've got an uncanny knack."

Both of her brows shot up with skepticism. "I don't like your tone. Was that a crack?"

With a tired smile, he dropped a brotherly arm about her thin shoulders, suggesting, "You're the mind reader. You tell me."

TESS SQUIRMED, thinking of her own duplicity. How could she have succumbed to her weakness for Cord now? She was a grown woman, for heaven's sake! What was she, some kind of masochist, determined to hurt herself in the worst possible way?

After writhing around in Cord's arms all afternoon, her body had radiated with a near terminal gratification. And it had all been because of Cord's incredible sexual mastery. Then she'd had to look up and see Nolan, steadfast and loyal, waiting for her on the dock. She felt like some philandering sailor with a lover in every port. It wasn't a good feeling. What was worse, it was lousy to be so trusted and yet be so grossly unworthy.

She berated herself unmercifully all the time she was showering and changing, then all through dinner. Her self-flagellation continued even now, as she sat listening to Etta and Ella Inch romping exuberantly through a piano and accordion duet: a medley of songs from the movie *Saturday Night Fever*.

Tess didn't know which was distressing her more, the bizarre rendition of "Stayin' Alive," which sounded strangely similar to a Bavarian polka, or the fact that Cord passed her skeptical looks whenever their eyes chanced to meet. Actually, if pressed to be starkly truthful, she knew which distressed her most. Those damned, doubting blue eyes. There was no humor in them. Only a dark challenge.

She knew what he was thinking—that she was near hysteria in her effort to be a charming mistress of ceremonies, as well as Nolan's idea of a delightful companion. So what if he was right, she groused inwardly, rubbing her temples. He didn't have to keep telling her so with every piercing glance. How she chose to live her life was none of his business!

She had a pounding headache and wanted nothing more than a deep drag on a cigarette and a warm bed. She hated these impromptu talent fests. She hated Nolan's delight in seeing her in charge. But, most of all, she hated Cord Redigo and his annoying know-it-all attitude.

When the Inch sisters paused to accept polite applause, Tess noticed that Cord was leaving the room. She felt a surge of emotion—whether it was relief or regret she was unable to determine. How muddleheaded she'd become since he'd walked back into her life. She couldn't even decipher her own feelings anymore!

Well, she didn't have time to wrestle with the problem now, she had to get up and be bubbly and witty and introduce the Inch sisters' next offering. She flipped her note card and scanned it for an instant as the clapping died away. It read: "A medley from the musical *Hair*." She stifled a sigh as she put on her best aren't-we-having-fun smile.

Cord stalked out of the inn and took in a gulp of air. It didn't make him feel any better. He scowled up at the stars as he strode angrily out to the end of the patio, his mind returning to the way Tess had looked minutes ago—so vulnerable, her eyes frantic, yet her face a fragile, convivial mask. He wondered why he was the only one who could see how miserable she was in her carefree-hostess role.

She was a lovely woman, but she wasn't a born entertainer. She wanted peace and an ironic sort of secure freedom, but life had given her work, worries, obligations . . . and a boyfriend who had the imagination of a dead flounder. Cord had half a mind to tell the idiot to buy a book on How to Be the Life of the Party and leave Tessa Jane alone. Why couldn't Nolan see that, given a choice, she'd much prefer to sit in a corner and read, or go outside and fly one of her kites. There wasn't the slightest hint of ham in that woman, and it pained Cord to see her struggle so in a role she detested.

It also pained him to see Nolan so satisfied with the situation as it stood. Cord ground out a blasphemy, not wanting to feel this odd brotherly protectiveness for Tess. He ran a hand through his hair, realizing that there was nothing brotherly about his feelings for Tessa Jane Mankiller. She might not be his type—blond and leggy and worldly-wise—but she had every bit of what a woman needs to make a man glad he's a man.

He thought of that afternoon, of Tess's amazing abandon in his arms, and felt himself go cold with the thought that he'd never know that elation again.

Suddenly he was consumed by a hunger that was so painful that he winced. Nostrils flaring, he muttered, "To hell with her," and headed off the patio along the winding path in the garden.

After barely a dozen steps, he found himself thinking about her eyes and the look he'd seen there that had sent him bounding from the parlor moments ago. His anger abated. He wanted to leave her the hell alone. This tenderness he was feeling now—pity, sympathy, whatever it was—he didn't like it, didn't want to feel it. She'd as much as told him to go to the devil this afternoon. Why couldn't he take the message to heart and ignore the need in her eyes?

Why, too, couldn't he resist the sweet-sexy pull of her feminine allure? Mary would scoff loud and long if she could read his thoughts right now. But he really didn't fall into the sack with every willing female who stepped across his path. Besides the fact that he wasn't the total rounder that Mary made him out to be, indiscriminate sex just wasn't a good idea in today's society. But there was something about Tess that made him forget good intentions and solid logic.

He'd vowed that he wouldn't put a hand on the lady, because that was very clearly the way she'd wanted it. And it had astonished him when she'd come on to him the way she had. Dammit to hell. He balled his fists. He couldn't believe he'd stumbled all over himself to get her to bed, so eager to make her cry out with delight, to hear her sighs of satisfaction, her whimpers of pleasure.

What the hell was his problem lately? He strode down the steps to the dock, angry with himself for doing this. He told himself grimly that whatever wonderful thing had happened between them that afternoon was water under the bridge. Why couldn't he turn his back and walk away? He took another two steps before he stopped, scanning the starry sky through eyes narrowed in a stony scowl.

Maybe it was because he'd already turned his back on her, once. Maybe. Anyway, for whatever obscure reason, he was on his way to the cruiser to retrieve his guitar. He couldn't stand to see Tess being Miss Merry Mistress of Ceremonies if it was so abhorrent to her.

He hadn't played his guitar for an audience in quite a while, but he figured he could do as well as Etta and Ella. Even in his foul mood he couldn't help but grin wryly. Hell! Two fighting cats on a back fence could do as well as Etta and Ella. That is, if they could fight in a polka rhythm.

A most singular interpretation of "The Age of Aquarius" ended with a galumphy little pirouette by Etta as she pressed her bellows together for the final chord. Moderate applause followed. Tess inhaled shakily, nervous to the point of giddiness. She was about to go into her own portion of the evening's entertainment, a recitation of poetry. She wasn't that great at it, but her efforts were always met with appropriate enthusiasm.

She looked around searching for Quillan Quimby, who she was sure would enjoy this. She couldn't find his among the sea of faces in the parlor. Deciding he must be on shore watch, she stood and straightened her skirt.

She had chosen to dress demurely in beige linen, half hoping she'd melt into the beigeness of the drawing room. She wore a double-breasted jacket, a cream-colored blouse with a froth of lace embellishing the front of the stand-up collar, a trumpet skirt and matching pumps. At the last minute, she'd even tucked her long hair into a neat bun at her nape.

She suspected her choice of clothing reflected a psychological desire to appear wholesome—though she was acutely aware that both she and at least one other person at the inn knew exactly what kind of wayward wanton she truly was.

She grimaced but hid the expression behind a mild clearing of her throat. The applause was entirely gone by the time she'd walked up to stand beside the glistening grand piano. She smiled sweetly, wishing she were some place less nerve-racking—such as over Niagara Falls on a fraying tightrope—and tried to recall the first line of Thomas Traherne's "Eden."

She was beaming outwardly. Inwardly, she was a tangled wreck. She began, "And now ladies and gentlemen, I'd like to—"

"No need to introduce me, Miss Mankiller," came Cord's deep voice. He strode toward her, looking incredibly sexy in well-worn jeans, faded in all the right places, and a rust-and-navy plaid shirt, the sleeves rolled up to reveal bronze muscle. His crooked smile was as winning as the night he was pronounced Broken Arrow High's "Mr. Charisma." "I think everybody here knows who I am."

By the time he'd finished speaking, he was beside her, his tangy after-shave assailing her nostrils and making her stomach lurch with unwanted memories. Tearing her gaze from his face, she realized for the first time that he was carrying a richly polished guitar. She had to work hard to keep her mouth from gaping in surprise. She blinked back up to stare at him, her face a frozen question.

He grinned down at her, but his smile cooled before it reached his eyes. It was evident that he was irritated with her, but she was sure she was the only person in the room who could see it.

"I thought it was about time for a down-home singalong," he explained, taking her elbow and forcing her with a gentle but determined pressure into a sitting position on the piano bench. Propping a silver-tipped boot on the bench, he turned toward the gathered guests and said, "I take requests." He grinned irrepressibly, and Tess hated the way the flash of teeth affected her.

He kidded, "Just don't ask me to sit down."

There was a ripple of laughter before Fred Summerfield asked, "Do you know Hank Williams's 'Hey, Good Lookin''?"

Cord winked. "Was practically weaned on it."

He strummed a few cords on the guitar before he began to sing the tune. His full-bodied voice held none of the familiar Hank Williams twang, and Tess felt the melody flow through her like warm syrup. She found herself relaxing as she watched his rugged profile, the tiny smile lines at the corner of his eyes, the sun-streaked waves of hair mussed by the evening wind. She especially enjoyed her close-up view of the cording and bunching of the muscles in his forearms as he strummed, his playing as mellow and provocative as his voice.

It didn't take long for the delighted gathering to join in, and some enthusiastic guests even began clapping to the beat. Tess would have preferred that they refrain, for they drowned out the subtleties of Cord's performance. She glanced around the room. The thirty-odd guests seemed completely enthralled. Even Etta and Ella had rapture written on their flushed pixie faces. Tess had to admit reluctantly that Cord was the picture of the Western hero—except he wasn't wearing a ten-gallon hat, but she decided it would be a sin to cover up that mass of silky hair.

Her fingers tingled as she recalled the feel of those golden strands against her hands, her breasts, her stomach. She clenched her fists in her lap, trying to choke the thought from her mind. She zeroed in on the singing, vowing to concentrate on the words of the new song that had just been requested.

Twenty minutes later, she was laughing with the rest of the audience as Cord related some of the more comical—if painful—experiences of his youth on a cattle ranch. Finally, with one last request from, of all people, Etta Inch, who was apparently a woman of eclectic musical taste, Cord began to sing a plaintive ballad.

Tess was very impressed not only by the range of Cord's voice but also by the sultry nuances he added to the words as he sang about a broken heart from a man's viewpoint, and how even a strong man can be devastated by a lost love.

In an instrumental segment, Cord hummed a sad, haunting accompaniment, making Tess shiver with tender emotion. She had to shake herself to regain proportion. Cord was merely singing a request, not pouring out his own feelings about being rejected. Lord in heaven, Cord Redigo, of all people, had no earthly idea of what being rejected was like!

Still, even as she tried to be stern and no-nonsense about the man, she couldn't help but soften a little. Once again, he was gouging at her emotional weak spot. This time he was doing much, much more for her than merely fixing her a dinner, he was taking responsibilities from her shoulders and transferring them to his own broad ones—and very successfully, too.

As he clung to the final, sweet note, Tess found herself holding her breath along with the rest of the audience. He sang like an angel—or a devil bent on beguiling. Whichever, she cautioned herself *never* to be alone with this man and his guitar. A little voice whispered that he'd had no guitar this afternoon, so she amended her resolve. She'd better not be alone with him ever, period.

When the applause began, his crooked smile blossomed slowly. To Tess's dismay, her cheeks warmed at the sight of it. She found herself on her feet, applauding loudly with the rest of the appreciative audience. Cord didn't turn her way at all, and she felt a rush of regret about that. She didn't blame him for ignoring her. Maybe—just maybe—he had felt slightly rejected today. His ego might have been bruised a bit—certainly not much, she was sure.

The audience had gathered round to congratulate him. Tess crossed her arms and watched him as he talked casually to his admirers. He was certainly a charmer, that man. There was probably a support group somewhere she ought to join for women who'd been snared by that fatal allure, only to discover that he hadn't meant anything by it. He just oozed it, like a maple tree oozes sap. She wondered where the national headquarters for Cord Redigo Anonymous was, then decided she was probably it.

A melancholy smile lifted her lips. She had an urge to hug Cord and strangle him at the same time. He'd been her first and only fantasy prince, and he'd also been her worst nightmare; but tonight he'd been a great help, and at this moment she felt no harsh emotion for him, only gratitude.

She cast one last look at him, the message "Thank you" in her eyes and her smile. But he didn't see it; his broad back was to her, no doubt on purpose. He was certainly *not needing* her with a vengeance tonight! She shook her head and walked toward the door. It was after ten and as good a time as any to call it quits for the night. She decided she'd have to make a point of telling Cord how good he had been at the very next opportunity, and how grateful she was. But right now, she didn't think he cared to hear a word from her.

Suddenly she spotted Nolan working his way through the crowd toward her and knew she'd have to shake him before she could escape to her room.

He caught her at the door, walking with her to the deserted kitchen where she poured them both a last cup of coffee.

"He was good, wasn't he," Nolan remarked after a quick sip.

Her gaze flew to him across the rim of her mug. She went ahead and took a scalding gulp before answering. "Uh-huh. I guess."

Nolan chucked her under the chin and grinned down at her. "I missed hearing your poetry, though. The way you act out George Herbert's 'The Temper'...I mean, when you swoop down for the line, 'Sometimes to Hell I fall', why it's just..." He frowned, searching for the word. "Oh, I don't know it's just..."

"A crime?" she helped.

He laughed. "Of course not. Really, you remind me of Shirley Temple with your cute gestures."

She had an urge to role her eyes in agony. "Don't let Shirley hear you say that. She might sue."

Nolan laughed again. It was a sound that was beginning to wear on her nerves. She tried to be fair. It wasn't Nolan's fault her nerves were raw. She smiled at him as best she could. "Well, Nolan, if you don't mind, I'm awfully tired. I think I'll go—"

"Sure, sure," he interrupted, taking her mug from her hand and setting it beside his on the counter. "First, I want to say something."

He moved up closer, and Tess swallowed, an inner voice warning her that this was going to be awkward.

"Tess," he began softly, his hands going about her waist, "You know how I feel about you. I've told you often enough."

She stared up at him. Unable to speak, she nodded feebly.

"I love you, Tess." He kissed her upturned nose, and then pulled her against his chest as he murmured heatedly, "Marry me. I need you in my life."

She bit her lip, staring into the wine-colored hounds-tooth pattern of his sweater vest. He *needed* her. But could she stand being needed the way he needed her, even for the security he was offering?

"Darling?" he whispered after a long moment. "I hope no news is good news."

She lifted arms weighed down by regret and pressed him gently away. Smiling tremulously up at his expectant face, she hedged, "Nolan, you've taken me quite off guard. . . ."

He touched her hot cheek with fingers that felt like ice. "After three proposals in two years, I would think you'd be getting pretty blasé about the question."

She felt a stab of pity, and stood on tiptoe to kiss his jaw. "Never blasé, Nolan." She stepped away. "But you know how the inn is—financially, I mean. . . ."

He smiled down at her, but the smile was only mildly successful. "That's why I'm still here on a Sunday night. I'm surprised you didn't ask me why I hadn't gone back to Burlington. You've seemed a little distracted lately."

She started. It was Sunday night? She'd forgotten to notice the days slipping by since Cord Redigo had sashayed back into her life. "Oh, I'm—I guess I've been preoccupied . . . with business. Uh, why are you still here?"

"The books. Remember, it's that time again, love."

He was right, she realized. And she also realized that she'd half-promised him that he'd have her final answer after he'd gone over the books this month. She'd told him that in a rash moment after putting him off yet again, several months ago. Now she would have no further options; Nolan had been more than patient. She smiled weakly. "Of course it is, Nolan. The books. Naturally, I remember."

"I thought you might be able to tell me you'd marry me before I had to prove to you that the inn is running in the black."

She blanched at the note of hurt she detected in his tone. Feeling terrible, she took his hand. "It's just a couple of days, Nolan." She manufactured a smile. "What's a little proof between close, close friends."

He seemed heartened by the idea that he'd have his answer in a few days. Sighing audibly, he squeezed her hand with both of his. "You know you can twist me around your pretty finger, don't you? I suppose I can wait."

She lowered her eyes, too cowardly to meet his devoted gaze.

He kissed her cheek before whispering, "A couple of days, sweetheart."

His footsteps grew distant, and she heard the kitchen door swing open at his touch. Unmoving, she listened to the metallic squeak of the hinges as the door swung back and forth in smaller and smaller arcs until it had stilled.

She crushed her hands together, feeling a little sick. Why couldn't she tell Nolan yes? He'd waited a long time for her. It wasn't fair to keep putting him off just because she felt nothing earthshaking for him. Their love could grow, couldn't it?

She lifted her gaze from her clenched hands to peer at the counter where Nolan's mug nudged hers. She suddenly had to move, to do something, anything. Snatching up the mugs, she walked to the sink and set them down, turning on the hot water spigot.

Cord was just a man like any other, she told herself. What she felt for him was merely an inconvenience, an odd chemical thing of no real importance, a perverse, buzzing little demon that needed to be brushed away like a bothersome fly.

He wasn't speaking to her, and that was just fine. She'd obviously succeeded in swatting him away this afternoon. She was lucky to be out from under.

She winced at the vision her unfortunate word choice conjured up. With a distracted flourish, she squirted some dish soap into the water. In two days, she'd accept Nolan's proposal, and all would be right with the world. Cord would go his way, and she and Nolan would go theirs. She grabbed a sponge and began to scrub a mug as though it was encrusted with rust. The idea of Cord exiting her life was very appealing, very satisfying, exactly what she wanted.

She gritted her teeth, leaning into her work. The mug suddenly broke in her hand, startling and confusing her. Where was product quality these days? Where had pride in one's work gone? Why, she sniffed, was she reduced to tears over a few ounces of ruined crockery?

8

TESS DABBED AT HER EYES and then wiped her hands on the kitchen towel, glad, at last, to be free to go up to bed. When Mary Cash appeared inside the kitchen door, her heart sank. Relatives of Cord Redigo were high on her list of people she didn't want to run into. She tried to put on a businesslike smile. "Why hello, Mary." She draped the towel over its bar, before asking, "What can I do for you?"

Mary smiled weakly and walked forward. "Nothing, hon. I hope I'm the one who can do something for you."

Tess was too tired for riddles. "I'm afraid I don't—"

Mary interrupted with a curt laugh. "I know that. And I'm glad to hear you don't. Cord already told me how you fought him off this afternoon."

Tess's eyes widened. She opened her mouth to ask exactly what Mary meant, but before she could speak, Mary went on, "I know I'm an awful busybody and should keep my mouth shut, but I like you, Tess, and I have a feeling you're just a little attracted to my libidinous cousin."

"Why, I—" Startled by Mary's directness, Tess couldn't form a coherent thought, let alone voice the denial that she wanted to scream out.

Mary shook her head, sighing loudly. "Old Cord's dashing and charming and all that muck." She walked closer, closing the gap between them. "And because he is, I feel it's my duty to ward off problems before they happen, if I can. Don't let him talk you into anything—or out of anything, if you understand my subtleties." She paused, smiled to herself and added, "Course, I've never been accused of being overly subtle."

"I'm sure you mean well, Mary," Tess began. "But you're mistaken about my attraction to your cousin." The lie tasted bitter in her mouth. "You see, I have a very sweet boyfriend in Nolan. I assure you, your cousin may be attractive, but he's not God's gift to women." She concluded a little tartly, "I'd rather not discuss him, if you don't mind."

Mary blinked at the edge to Tess's clipped request. "Well, it's just that I gathered you two once had some sort of relationship, and I was worried that—"

"Don't worry about it," Tess interrupted. "That was years ago and there was absolutely no relationship. We had a difference of opinion then, and I'm afraid we still share that difference. In truth, I really don't care very much for your cousin." She was ashamed of herself for blurting out such an unkind piece of fiction about Cord to his own cousin, but she was wound up so tightly that if she didn't drop to the floor and start screaming and kicking it would be a miracle. She bit her tongue to keep her mouth shut.

Mary's expression was skeptical to say the least. "Well, honey, if you say so. I hope I didn't upset you. Like I said, I'm a dyed-in-the-wool meddler, and since

I know how dedicated Cord is to his work . . ." She shrugged. "Well, there never seemed to be any room for a permanent woman in his life. He's a workaholic and a little strange about fish, but I love him.

"I know how he affects women, and I don't want him to hurt nice young ladies like yourself. Even though the dear boy'd never do it intentionally." She patted Tess's shoulder. "But since you don't even like the guy, let's pretend this chat never happened. Okay?"

Tess nodded dumbly.

"Fine." She inclined her head. "Anything else you want to get off your chest?"

"No . . . no, thanks. I appreciate your concern."

Mary nodded curtly. "Would you mind not telling Cord I said anything? He'd kick my skinny rear all the way back to Burlington. For some reason he thinks his business ought to be private." Her devilish grin was so reminiscent of Cord's that Tess blanched at the sight.

Mary laughed crisply. "Men can be such trusting fools."

Tess thought of Nolan and bit the inside of her cheek.

With one more hearty pat on Tess's shoulder, Mary said, "Good night, hon. Give my regards to that sweet boyfriend of yours." She turned on her heel to go, but called back over her shoulder, "And keep your guard up."

THE NEXT DAY went by in a haze for Tess. She kept recalling Mary's final words. *"Keep your guard up."* She laughed out loud, drawing Kalvin's attention from his polishing. "Did ya say somethin' Ms Mankiller?" he asked, obviously perplexed.

She shook her head, slumping further into her paperwork. "No, Kalvin. I was just thinking out loud."

"Oh." He squinted at her for a minute and then went back to his work.

"Keep your guard up," Tess repeated mentally, squelching the urge to scoff out loud again. She shuffled papers, trying to concentrate on the bills. She failed. Cord Redigo had been noticeably absent all day. She had it on good authority that he was a very busy man, and it was painfully evident that he was being very busy avoiding her. As for Mary's warning to keep her guard up, well, considering Cord's hotfooted pursuit of her these past twenty-four hours, she might as well transfer her energies to a more urgent project . . . such as stuffing her head in a flowerpot.

"All done oiling the wood, Ms Mankiller. Can I quit for supper, now?"

Tess looked up with a start as Kalvin rose from his kneeling position beside her wooden file cabinets.

"Oh. Sure." She looked at her watch simply to be doing something. "It's after seven. Go eat."

He grinned and loped out of her office without another word.

She stretched, then dropped her pen into the brass cup on her desk. Standing and surveying her cluttered desk, she decided to leave it. She was not ordinarily one to leave a messy desk, but today she just couldn't care less about neatness and order. She didn't know what her problem was, exactly. Maybe all she needed was a shower.

By the time she'd trudged up the stairs to her room she knew that her true need at the moment wasn't a shower; it was a cleansing talk with Cord. She still felt guilty about yesterday. But she'd had a lot of time during the long hours of the night to think about everything, and she'd come to some conclusions that Cord needed to hear.

She planned to get her gripe off her chest, and this was as good a time as any. Marching past her own room, she pivoted at his door and knocked. The sound her knuckles made against the maple slab was more timid than she'd planned for it to be.

When at first there was no response, she breathed a sigh. Part of her didn't really want this confrontation. She'd just turned to go when she heard Cord say, "Come in."

She swallowed. Her resolve had slipped a notch when she'd heard the sound of his voice. She reached for the doorknob and then drew back, fidgeting with the spaghetti strap of her white bodice that had slid off her shoulder. When she'd replaced it, she adjusted the open-front black jacket with its tiny white polka dots, wishing there was a long row of buttons to fasten. When she'd ordered the jumpsuit from the mail-order catalogue, she hadn't realized she'd have to go braless in it. And somehow, the idea of going braless in front of Cord Redigo seemed an extremely foolhardy thing to do.

She reached for the doorknob again, but it moved before she could grasp it. She looked up, surprised, as Cord pulled the door wide. He appeared every bit as surprised as she.

"Well, hello," he offered, his brows lifting quizzically. "I don't remember ordering anything from room service."

He didn't look particularly overjoyed to see her, but on the plus side, he didn't spit at her. She wondered what five minutes would bring, after she'd said her piece. "We don't have room service," she ventured, trying out her voice, which sounded normal.

He crossed his arms, watching her closely. "I know."

She cleared her throat. It was time to get to the meat of the matter. "Cord. I'd like to talk to you."

He took his time surveying her attire before asking, "Do you want to come in or will the hallway do?"

"Well, I—I really don't think the hallway..."

He pursed his lips, his gaze leveled on her as he stepped back.

However meager his invitation had been, she accepted it, closing the door at her back. "May we sit?"

He indicated the room. It was small, with few amenities. "Would you prefer the bed or the chair?"

She frowned. "The chair," she told him firmly.

When she was seated in the tall wingback chair, she tugged her jacket to a more modest position over her breasts while he was taking a seat opposite her at the foot of his bed.

Once seated, he waited quietly as she crossed her legs and then uncrossed them, trying to think of how to word what she had to say.

He watched her with a curious frown, looking all too relaxed, with his knees wide, close enough to touch the outside of hers. His hands, fingers spread, rested on the patchwork quilt, propping him up.

Tess noticed that his hair was slightly damp from a shower. She could detect the fragrance of soap, but no cologne. He was wearing gray linen slacks, gray deck shoes and a gray sweatshirt that looked soft but manly. She noticed the scent of leather, now, too. She liked the combination of bath soap and leather, clean and extremely masculine.

"What did you want to talk about, Tessa Jane?" Cord finally asked, making her jump.

After regrouping her wits, she defiantly jutted her chin at him. "You're not going to like it."

His lips quirked sardonically, as if to say, So what else is new?

When he didn't actually voice the sarcastic question, she rushed on. "You—you were very unfair to take advantage of me on the boat yesterday." She tossed her hair back over her shoulder, daring him with a narrowed, angry stare to deny her charge.

His eyes widened slightly for just an instant. But he didn't offer any defense.

Trying to ignore the flash of incredulity in his gaze, she hurried on, "I told you, in a moment of weakness, about my need to be not needed." Highly agitated, she got to her feet and found herself trapped between his spread legs. Deciding to use her captivity to her advantage, she poked him in the shoulder. "It was small and cruel of you to use that knowledge to seduce me."

Cord lowered his silver-tipped lashes but said nothing. His lack of defense seemed to give her argument strength, so she pressed on, deciding to tell him what she had originally planned to say when she'd come to his room the last time, on Sunday afternoon.

"And furthermore—" she poked "—I want you to cut out your interference with Nolan and me. Life has taught me that love is a trade-off. If you want something, you have to give something back. That is, if you're not a total egotist."

His gaze had grown steady and thoughtful as he listened. Unwilling to maintain eye contact with a man who was now filled with obvious pity, she quickly dropped her gaze and paced away from him.

Reaching the wall, she whirled on him again. She didn't want pity from him. She wanted peace! *Damn him!*

Without thinking, she lashed out, "I gave something to you once. And all I got for my trouble was a ride home and a lecture!" Her voice broke on the last word. Hating her show of weakness, she spun away to collect herself.

When she turned back, he was towering over her, too near for clear thinking. She cast tormented eyes up to meet his and was stunned by the stark unhappiness in his face.

"I failed you, Tessa Jane." He spoke her name gently and took her hand in his. "I was a bastard, but I was a kid then, too, confused and upset. I'm really sorry I couldn't give you what you wanted. But I didn't know you. How could I love you?"

Reluctantly, she saw the logic in his hushed remark. As he led her to sit with him on the edge of the bed, she examined his strong, angular face, recalling the heavenly feel of those lips against hers and wishing the image would disappear forever.

When they were seated, their knees touching, he pulled both of her hands on his lap. "Did you know that you're the only virgin I've ever made love to?"

She stared dumbly.

"The only blot on my record." His chuckle was bitter, self-deprecating. "You see, what I do in the Indian Ocean is important work. Even in high school I knew my chosen career would require all my energy, leaving no room for entanglements."

A bleak expression came into her eyes and Cord felt that same, odd tenderness he'd felt toward her last night when he'd gone after his guitar. Unable to resist the urge, he kissed her forehead. When she'd realized his intention, she'd drawn back, but only slightly.

With his lips still brushing her fragrant skin, he told her honestly, "I disagree that love has to be a tradeoff. I know it's none of my business, but we've been through enough together that I've earned the right to tell you how I feel."

As their gazes touched again, he warned gently, "Don't give up your dreams of freedom for some nebulous concept of security, Tessa Jane. You won't be happy in the long run."

He looked so genuinely concerned that she softened, amazed that with a brief kiss and a few supportive words, he could turn her to putty.

Her smile was slow and reticent. "I didn't mean to get back on that old hayride thing. Really..." she mumbled. "I mean, yesterday just got me so upset, and when Nolan—" She stopped herself. She had no intention of saying anything about his marriage proposal. Not after the speech Cord had just made. "What I'm trying to say is, I know you're not a bad guy. It's just that I'm feeling guilty and it's eating me up. Last night was tough for me, facing Nolan and being, well, being 'up' and all. . . ."

"I noticed," Cord cut in, the mildness in his expression evaporating. "And just why did you feel you needed to be up for Nolan? Didn't you hear anything I just said? Why can't the man ever be up for you?"

She frowned. "This is different. I'm the manager of the inn. It's my job to be up."

"No, it's not. It's your job to make sure sewage doesn't back up into the bathtubs and that the staff isn't made up of serial killers. It's not your job to be Bert Parks."

She blanched. "What are you talking about? I'm just being what I need to be to—"

"Get approval?" he asked, cutting her off.

She stared, confused. "No. I . . ."

His laughter was harsh. "You're using people, too, you know. That's why you work so hard all the time—to get approval. Why in hell do you want the whole damned world's approval, anyway?"

She jerked her hands from his, lashing back, "Well, I'll tell you one thing, I'm certainly not looking for *your* approval!"

"Fine," he retorted. "You don't need my approval. With or without it, you're still a very worthwhile person."

His defusing comment took Tess completely by surprise. She'd always thought of herself as not quite worthwhile. Her mother had gone off and died on her, and all Tess's work and devotion hadn't been enough to console her father, who'd drunk himself to death.

Her aunt Jewel, who at the time had been rapidly going blind, had needed Tess, and appreciated her taking over the floundering inn. But Tess had been well aware of the fact that she had been thrust on her aunt, there being no other relative to take her in. So she'd tried hard to be worthy of her aunt's generosity, working night and day to earn her love. Funny, until just this minute, she'd never considered the possibility that she was using people, in a way, to satisfy her own need to be loved.

Cord relented, smiling at her. "You're a classy woman, Tess. I respect you. I like you, but, sweetheart, I don't need you."

There was a lovely irony to Cord's declaration. He didn't need her. Something like sunshine began to glow deep inside Tess's breast, radiating outward to warm her limbs and make her eyes shimmer with gratitude. She found herself smiling back at him, really smiling. "Some people might say that was an insulting remark," she told him quietly.

His gaze wandered over her face before he began to stroke her cheek. "For what it's worth, I didn't say I didn't want you."

With his husky rejoinder, her smile faded and she abruptly resumed the struggle with her jacket.

He was struck by the brief shadow of vulnerability he glimpsed in her eyes, and felt himself tremble involuntarily. In spite of all his honorable intentions, he drew her to him. Her sweet, sad lips promised undeniable pleasures. "I hate it when the things I say make you unhappy," he whispered, his voice raspy with regret.

Before she had time to respond, he brushed her neck with his lips.

She sat there motionless, lost in the mesmerizing power of his clever, ravenous mouth. Her lips opened in a silent oh. She could feel herself melting at his touch, but she had no desire to move away. Still, she tried to grasp at the last remnants of common sense.

"I—" she swallowed "—knew it was a mistake to wear this outfit," she half sighed, half moaned. "I knew it would come to no good to face you in anything less than a suit of armor."

"Why did you, then?" he queried, the timbre of his voice lower.

"I don't—" she groaned, unable to finish. The barest touch of his lips at the corner of her mouth made her feel woozy. Her whimper of denial and desire was swallowed up by Cord's hungry mouth as he took possession of hers with a sudden sly ferocity that left her shaking. Nothing mattered now but the distressing yet exquisite pleasure he was coaxing from her as his tongue laid claim to the intimate recesses of her mouth.

She moaned, helpless to intercede in her own defense, as he slid the collar of her jacket away and slowly trailed his lips down to nibble at her shoulder.

He brushed her hands away from their death grip on her jacket and boldly cupped a breast, his thumb rubbing the taut bud of her nipple. "If you wore this just to drive me crazy, Tessa Jane, you've succeeded," he said, his voice breathless.

Some nasty little imp in the back of her mind was tittering with laughter. It knew that Tessa Jane Mankiller had selected this jumpsuit with special care this morning. It also knew that Tessa Jane Mankiller was the foolish, perhaps even deliberate, author of her own destruction. Why hadn't she caught on before it was too late?

Cord had taken the slender strap in his teeth and was slipping it off her shoulder as his hands busied themselves with the zipper at her back. By the time the other strap had been lowered, Tess was lying on her back.

As gently as if he were folding back the wrapping on a precious gift, Cord lowered her bodice to display her breasts. Dipping his head, he placed a sweet kiss in the valley between them, paying silent homage to her beauty. Tess responded with as much charged energy as if he'd ripped her bodice open.

With a pained little cry, she wrapped her arms about him, pressing his face into her softness, wanting him to feast on her until she was completely devoured. As he enjoyed her womanly offerings, she relished the various textures of the man, the juxtaposition of soft and hard, the softness of his sweatshirt, the hardness of muscle beneath.

A flush of desire diffused her body. She could tell that Cord, too, was deeply affected. He felt feverish, tense beneath her hands. She could practically feel his nerves jumping under his skin.

Witnessing his arousal ignited all the erotic emotions she'd been working to control. It would do no good to waste energy damning the little imp within her that had orchestrated her latest downfall. She realized now that nothing on earth could have prevented her from knowing this man's touch again. Chemistry being what it was, she was becoming resigned to the idea that there was no hope for sane thinking while Cord Redigo was within touching distance.

She gasped as his teeth teased a nipple, and she licked her lips in concert with the movement of his tongue. Her core was glowing, throbbing mercilessly with hot need.

She ran her hands through his hair, and then in a fit of bravado she would never have believed possible, she caught and held the silky stuff, pulling his head up so that he was forced to look into her face.

She gazed up at him. His eyes were softly glazed with desire, his expression beautiful even in his confusion about what she had in mind. Suddenly, the little imp within her surfaced. With a knowing smile she whispered, "I have a news bulletin."

Cord looked worried. She couldn't bear the uncertainty in his eyes. It was too cruel a thing to do to a man at this advanced stage in the act of passion. Cupping his head in her hands, she assured him, "Evidently hell froze over a couple of times today." She drew his face up and brushed his lips lightly with hers, adding, "Take off your clothes."

Hearing her husky order, his eyes lit like twin devils. "Yes, ma'am," he obliged just above a whisper, enfolding her for one more lingering kiss. Finally, he rolled away and tugged the sweatshirt off over his head. In rapt excitement she watched the play of muscles across his chest as he tossed the garment on the chair. When he began to unbutton his trousers, she brushed away his hands. "I'll take over from here."

She pressed him to his back, then giggled at the surprise in his expression. With one quick movement, she slid the rest of the way out of her jumpsuit and kicked off her sandals. Clad only in bikini panties, she straddled his thighs and began to undo the slacks.

Seconds later, she'd helped him slip out of both trousers and underwear. The degree of his arousal was galvanizing. Tess grinned slyly down at his expectant face. Reveling in the wonder of being a woman, she bent forward.

In words that were almost a prayer, he asked, "Are you going to—"

"Teach you to take," she murmured, and her lips found their objective.

His wistful groan of pleasure gladdened her beyond all her expectations.

TESS STIRRED, not quite opening her eyes to the morning. The alarm hadn't gone off, but she had the strangest feeling she'd just been kissed...on the thigh. She felt it again, but higher this time. Her eyes flew wide when the full realization hit her groggy brain of how, and with whom she'd fallen asleep last night!

She sat up, unaware that her naked breasts were swaying tantalizingly for Cord's hungry perusal. He smiled down at her, his eyes drinking her in. "Good morning," he fairly sang, placing a wicker bed tray across her lap. "I hope you like scrambled eggs." His eyes twinkled as he lowered his head to kiss the tip of each breast before he backed away. "I told Sugar I wanted to eat in my room this morning, so she dug up a tray for me. Didn't think it'd be safe to ask her to dig up two." He grinned the grin of a sated man. "Thought she might wonder who else was eating breakfast in my bed."

He looked wonderful in the buttercup light of early morning. His sky-blue flannel shirt and worn jeans that tugged enticingly at hip and thigh hid little of his manliness, and she relived the glory of his nude body. Forcing the picture from her mind, she tried to speak sensibly. "I can't eat scrambled eggs . . . naked."

He sat down beside her and smoothed her hair back from her ear so that he could nuzzle a tempting lobe. "Humor me. I love you this way. All the prim little innkeeper is gone when you take off your clothes." He made a sexy growling sound in his throat. "Baby, if I never see you in clothes again, it'll suit me just fine."

She blanched, tugging a sheet up to conceal her breasts. "Don't call me 'baby,' Cord."

He sat back, but continued to stroke the inside of her wrist with his thumb. "Why not? I called you that several times last night."

She cast her eyes down at her tray. "Never mind. I guess 'baby' is okay . . . under certain limited circumstances."

"Good." He lifted the lid on her breakfast and stood. "I promise, I won't call you baby in public."

When their gazes met again, she couldn't keep herself from smiling. His grin was so wicked, so undeniable that it made her pulse flutter into high gear. Stifling a shiver at the exhilarating recollection of their night together, she patted the bed. "Join me. I don't usually eat much breakfast."

He poured some coffee into the mug. "I'll share your java with you. Sugar forced a couple of cinnamon rolls on me while I was in the kitchen. She was a little surprised when I still wanted eggs, bacon, toast, juice and coffee in my room."

Tess couldn't suppress a laugh. "The way Virge eats, I doubt that Sugar will be the least bit suspicious."

He handed her the mug, telling her softly, "You were a wild woman last night, Tessa Jane. Hell may have been a cold place, but it was plenty hot in here."

She was in the midst of taking a sip. With widened eyes, she lowered the mug to the tray and murmured, "Don't say that, Cord. I was a fool again. But I realize now that there is little I can do about the way I'm attracted to you."

His face grew serious. "That's not very flattering, honey. There's a lot we can do about it, and if last night was any indicator, every minute will be spectacular."

Tess exhaled slowly, dropping her gaze to the plate of cooling food. How wonderful it was to be here, feeling so uninhibited with Cord. It was almost frightening to be so at ease with him, so one with a man who was, by his own admission, not right for her. He was a vagabond. His work was his love, his life, his passion . . . at least his long-standing passion.

This nagging truth dimmed a little when he nuzzled the top of her head.

"What are you thinking, babe?" he murmured against her hair.

"Nothing," she fibbed weakly, forcing a small smile. "I was just wishing you'd asked for the eggs sunny-side up."

He chuckled. "I'll remember that for tomorrow."

Her breath caught in her throat. Could she possibly allow this to continue?

9

TESS SNUGGLED CLOSER in the crook of Cord's arm, and rubbed her palm across the blond haze of hair on his chest. She loved the texture of it, at the same time soft and rough against her skin. She inhaled. His scent was less distinct now. He smelled vaguely of flowers. She smiled to herself. No, that was her own perfume mingled intimately with Cord's scent. There was no separating the two anymore. They were one living being as far as her olfactory sense was concerned. What a nice idea.

When she sighed contentedly, he patted her hip beneath the sheet that swathed her. He, too, was covered modestly, but for one brazenly naked leg that he had drawn up to rest an elbow on so that he could more easily look down into her face.

"What are you thinking?" he asked her softly.

She drew her gaze from his chest and looked up, her eyes smiling. She didn't dare tell him what she was really thinking. Instead she asked him something that she'd been wondering about for years. "Are you sure you're part Osage Indian? You're so blond."

He chuckled and it tickled her cheek. "The last three generations of men in my family were all attracted to Nordic types."

"Oh . . ." She felt a little stab of hurt. Her eyes touched his tentatively, and the question slipped out before she could monitor what she was saying. "Then what are you doing with me, slumming, genetically speaking?"

"Tessa Jane," he admonished gently, as he brushed his lips against her hair. "Don't put yourself down."

He graced her with a soft smile. "As long as we're speaking physiologically, I was thinking how sexy you'd look lying in a teepee, that midnight hair splayed across a stack of wolf pelts." He smoothed a strand of the stuff from her forehead and kissed the spot, whispering, "No man with the good luck to spend the night with you, in a palace or a teepee, could possibly be slumming, genetically or otherwise."

She felt a surge of happiness rush through her and hugged him closer, dusting his jaw with a kiss. She knew she shouldn't do it; she knew it would ruin her mood, but she had to ask, "Tell me about your work, Cord." She didn't really want to hear how important it was, how necessary it was for him to travel so far away, but she figured she had to hear it. She had to face the reality of his life choices now, while they were lying naked together, so that when he left her, she'd be well aware of exactly where she stood in his life, and not expect him to ever be back.

"Now?" he asked, sounding amused.

"What better time?"

"Hmm." He appeared to think about it for a minute before he agreed. "I've never given a lecture to a naked woman. I'm not sure I can keep my mind on ichthyology."

"Maybe I can help you," she offered.

He arched a curious brow. "How?"

"I'll put on an overcoat," she teased, starting to move away from him.

"Never mind." He pulled her back down. "I'll manage."

"Good," she said, settling back within his embrace, "because I really do want to hear about your work."

"That's a lie, but it's a nice one." He traced her nose with one finger then kissed its tip before beginning. "My old friends, the coelacanths, first appeared on earth about 400 million years ago. That was before Champ." He winked, teasing her. "By studying them we may someday be able to shed light on a vital stage of evolution—namely, the time when creatures first wriggled from the water and walked on land, becoming ancestors of all land animals, including man."

"Fascinating," she said, smiling up at him, more in an enjoyment of his nearness than any real interest in the subject.

"Yeah, right."

She wrapped her arms around him and cuddled closer. "Please go on."

Nuzzling the top of her head with his jaw, he murmured, "Well, there's a lot more I have to learn. For instance, why have coelacanths remained virtually unchanged for aeons? What environmental conditions enabled these passive, sluggish creatures to survive for some thirty million generations?"

"And you have to be the man to find out?"

She felt his shrug. "I want to be the man."

"You will," she assured him, positive that he would. Cord Redigo was a winner, if she'd ever seen one. She felt a surge of pride just to know him. She somehow knew that she was holding a man who would, one day, be renowned in the annals of science.

"Tell me more about these precious fish of yours."

"Boring."

She toyed with a tuft of blond chest hair, curling it about her finger. "Tell me. I want to know."

He laid his hand across her arm, stroking it gently with his thumb. "If you insist, but I know something much more interesting we could be doing."

She giggled. "You're an animal."

"You should talk."

"Don't change the subject."

He exhaled. "Okay. First, coelacanths are relatively large—nearly six feet in length. The presence of two sets of paired fins on their underside indicates that these may have been the rudimentary legs, making them an extremely important find. Secondly, they're slow, awkward fish. Unable to compete for prey with most species, they retreated to depths where others couldn't survive for lack of food. We can only find the coelacanths at night and at depths of almost 550 feet, and only in the Indian Ocean. They move to even deeper and cooler water during the day."

"But you can't scuba dive that deep," she remarked. "Can you?"

"No. We have a two-man submersible. My partner, Hans, and I go down and study the coelacanths for eight-hour stretches. Did you know that those crazy fish do headstands on the ocean floor, and they swim backward, sometimes belly up?" He chuckled again, rubbing her arm as he spoke.

"Do they ever walk on their fins?" Tess asked, really interested, but not quite able to get her mind off Cord's soft stroking. He was a very physical person, and she loved that about him. Never in her life had anyone petted her lovingly that way.

"I've seen them rest against the sea bottom on their fins, but never walk. I have to admit that's been a bit of a disappointment," he murmured, adding with a slight smile, "But for every myth dispelled, there are many fascinating discoveries still to be made."

She looked up at him. "Are you talking about Champ?"

"Not specifically." He grinned. "Just myths in general."

"And you want to be the one to dispel the myths and make the discoveries?"

He nodded, his eyes soft. "Always have."

"Hmm." She had to admit that his work was important, and she also had to admit that it was truly a passion with him. He spoke of the fish as though they were close friends. She tried to keep from feeling depressed as she asked, "Didn't you say once that the coelacanth was thought to be extinct?"

"Uh-huh." He slid his hand up her arm, his knuckles grazing her breast. The casual touch caused a shock of pure pleasure to sing through her body.

"Scientists thought they'd been extinct for seventy million years, then in 1938 one was caught in a trawler's net and an alert naturalist spotted it. That coelacanth is now on display in the East London Museum in South Africa."

"And it was you who brought the first two live specimens back to the New York Aquarium."

He nodded.

"You must be proud."

He grinned down at her. "The word is *relieved*. I wasn't sure if they'd survive the flight."

Tess looked up at him, knowing that this man would very soon go out of her life and walk into the history books. She didn't really feel like teasing, but deciding it was better to tease than to cry, she taunted softly, "And you're a doubting Thomas about Champ when your precious coelacanth was also thought to be extinct? Isn't that a little narrow-minded for a scientist?"

Uninterested in a debate at the moment, Cord kissed her bare shoulder. "You may have a point," he murmured, his lips bedeviling her cool flesh.

There was a sharp rap at Cord's door, bringing him up, alert. "Who—"

"Hi ya, cuz. Sugar told me you were having breakfast in your room. Figured you'd be interested in the fisherman's photographs," Mary was chatting away as she pushed open the door, her eyes on a handful of pictures. "Just as you feared, a combination of atmospheric refraction and—" When she looked up, Cord had moved forward to try to protect Tess as best he could from the embarrassment of being caught in his bed.

Mary's expression changed from an irritated all-business squint to one of wide-eyed disbelief. "Lord," she prayed aloud, her agony theatrically evident. "Let me *not* be seeing what I'm seeing!"

"Thanks for dropping by, Mary," Cord said. "You may go now."

Mary leaned tiredly against the door as it clicked shut and groaned. "When Sugar said you were having breakfast in your room, I didn't think she meant Miss Mankiller."

"I don't mean to be rude, but—" Cord indicated the door with a jerk of his head.

Mary gave him a killing stare and then peered around him to look at Tess, who had shrunk down as far as she could into the pillows, wishing she were dead. Mary shook her head, her expression pained and sympathetic. "Sometimes I think hormones are more trouble than they're worth."

"Goodbye, Mary." The growled words were a thinly veiled threat.

"I'm going," she snapped, turning away. Then, with her hand on the knob, she turned back. "You want these pictures?"

"Mary," Cord began, his voice barely controlled. "When you're dead you'll still have enough wind to deliver your own eulogy!" He arched a brow meaningfully. "And that event may come sooner than you'd like."

She nodded largely. "So you don't want the pictures. Don't get testy. I'm going."

The last thing they heard before the door closed was Mary's louder than necessary exclamation, "*Oh, hel-loooo, Nolan!* Looking for me? Oh, *Tess!* Uh, haven't seen her since, er, my mind's a blank."

The door banged shut. Panicked green eyes shot to brooding blue ones before Tess deliberately withdrew her gaze. Her whole body was flaming with mortal humiliation. Nolan was knocking at her door and she was tangled in another man's sheets. Not only that, but her moral disintegration had been witnessed by a third party.

Feeling guilty and traitorous, she struggled to free herself from the chaos of Cord's bed. Without a backward glance, she padded a hasty retreat to her room.

Cord reached out to stop her, then drew his hand back. He scowled, watching her sweet, naked hips taunt him in her flight until she disappeared beyond the bathroom door. When she was gone, he flung his legs over the side of the bed and slumped forward, running his hands distractedly through his hair. What in hell had he been thinking when he'd reached for her? What, he wondered, in that mindless instant, had he thought he was going to say?

Twenty minutes later, Cord was on the *Coelacanth II*, roughly yanking on his wet suit. Mary had called him a short while before, not allowing him a word in edgewise, relating a very terse message. She'd told him that had he been "less erotically occupied or more modestly clothed" she would have been able to tell him what she'd come up there for—namely, that there had been some large blips on the sonar at about 100 feet out in the cove. Since she was fighting a lousy inner ear problem, Cord was their resident scuba diver. Would he set up the underwater camera in the cove, seeing as how it had a rich history of reported sightings?

She had quickly hung up, but not before she told him with hearty good humor, "Save some time for me, later, stud. When I've calmed down, we have to talk."

When she calmed down? He snorted out a sarcastic laugh. She'd be calmed down about the time hell froze over, and hell had been doing way too much freezing over in the past twenty-four hours for there to be much chance of it happening again.

He leaned against the railing and dragged on the black scuba pants, zipping the legs before grabbing up the top half of the suit. His thoughts turned to Tess. She didn't want to be needed, but there was something *she* needed. That was an unselfish love in her life. With an irritated tug on the waterproof material, he forced his arms into the tight sleeves, muttering a short oath.

He'd been selfishly enjoying the uninhibited way Tess expressed herself sexually. He'd always enjoyed women, but they hadn't been vulnerable in the way Tess was. They'd been sophisticated when it came to men like Cord, taking their pleasure while they could get it and expecting nothing more than a good time in return.

Tess wasn't casual about her attachments, especially sexual ones. He zipped up the front of his suit with a jerk. He was doing her harm by making love to her so casually, and it was unfair to her, probably as unfair as anything he'd ever done to a woman in his life.

Maybe love was a trade-off of sorts. So what if Nolan needed her spirit and drive in his life? What was so bad about that? Since Cord was single, obsessed with his profession and laboring under no desire to get married, what the hell right did he have to tell other people how to handle their personal relationships?

When he'd dragged on his fins and donned his tanks, he promised himself he'd back off and leave Tess to make her own decisions. And while he was backing off, he'd damn well better get his libido under control, too, and leave her alone. That idea pinched a little. Or was it the wet suit? He shook his head and grabbed his face mask.

As he rolled backward over the side of the boat, he visualized Mary's disgusted face before him. He doubted that assuring his cousin of his new resolve would save him the verbal thrashing she was planning for him. Maybe he could try strangling her before she could get out a condemning word. The idea was pleasant, and he mulled it over as he descended into the nebulous depths, hauling the camera equipment in its special basket. But what if he deserved her piercing accusations? After all, he recalled quite vividly who grabbed whom last night.

IT WAS NEARLY FIVE O'CLOCK when Tess finished up her myriad chores for the day. Having successfully sidestepped Nolan for most of that time, she hoped to have a few minutes of refuge with her new kite version of Champ, a plesiosaur. Her lips lifted in a rueful smile. She'd made her latest kite to Cord's specifications and the man didn't even believe in her monster!

What an idiot she was! And weak? She'd been smoking like a smoldering sofa all day. She hated herself for her lapse, or rather, lapses. She couldn't seem to give up smoking, and what was worse, she couldn't seem to steer clear of Cord who appeared to be another extremely addictive habit.

As the silken plesiosaur soared and quivered high above the lake, Tess's gaze dropped to scan the deck of the cabin cruiser. According to Quillan, Cord had been in and out of the water all day, having trouble with the camera equipment. He wasn't in sight and she wondered if he was diving deep under the water. The idea made her shiver with fear. What dangers lurking there were anybody's guess.

"Hello, sweetheart," Nolan remarked quietly, cutting through her train of thought. Spinning to face him, she almost lost hold of her kite line. "Oh!" she gasped. "Hello, Nolan."

"Can we talk?" he asked, his face hopeful.

"Of course." She smiled wanly and looped the line around the top bolt of her kite anchor a couple of times. The kite could fly itself for a while. She looked up to give Nolan her complete attention. She owed him that. "I'm all yours."

His eyes took on an optimistic gleam. "That sounds promising." Pulling her hand into his, he asked, "I thought you'd have an answer for me since the books are finished. And I might add, the inn is prospering nicely." He squeezed her fingers. "I told you it would be, didn't I?"

She nodded, gratified by *that* news, anyway. "Yes, you did, Nolan. And thanks for your able assistance for these past two years."

His stance became somehow wary, as if he were afraid of being knocked down. "That sounds a little like I'm being fired," he murmured.

She licked her lips, averting her gaze for an instant as she said, "Not if you don't want to be. It's just that . . ."

She couldn't voice the rejection. But she was rejecting him; she knew it now. There was no hope for the two of them ever getting together. Her intellect had been insisting for two years that Nolan would be a good husband, but her heart had quailed at the idea of spending the rest of her days and nights with this man in his secure, well-ordered home in nearby Burlington, Vermont. She sighed wearily.

After a long silence, Nolan let go of her hands. "I guess that's answer enough." He sounded dejected. Leaning down, he kissed her on the cheek, telling her through a long exhale, "I'd better be getting back to town. I've been neglecting my other clients."

She met his eyes regretfully, but when she did, Nolan smiled down at her with an unexpected degree of understanding. "I hope you find what you're looking for, Tess. I just hope it's not as elusive as your mythical Champ."

Before she had time to absorb his words, he'd turned to go. She watched him walk away, feeling very unhappy. She pondered his final words. Was it possible to have freedom and security, too? She doubted it. How could she be so crazy to think she could find love with no strings attached?

Still, as Nolan disappeared into the inn, she knew she'd made the right decision. A wave of relief rushed over her, proving once and for all that Nolan was not the right choice for her. It was better for him to be a little unhappy now than for them both to be miserable later.

She turned back and listlessly unwound her kite from its anchor. As she did so, she could see a dark figure appear at the stern of the boat and toss black fins on board before climbing up the ladder. He was tall and lean and glistened like gem-quality black coral. She dragged her eyes away, but her thoughts dwelt on what it might be like to dive down there, to swim deep beneath the surface of the lake with Cord by her side....

Lord! Under the surface of a cold, murky lake was the last place she could ever imagine wanting to be! Snatching irritably at the line, she began pulling in her kite. She needed to get away—anywhere—anywhere she couldn't see Cord. She choked back a ragged sob as an unwanted, damnable realization flashed in her mind. She was in love with him.

She'd read somewhere that small passions died with absence, but grand passions only grew larger. She had to face the truth now. Her passion for Cord was of the very grandest kind, one she would never get over. And that being true, she was a fool, of the very grandest kind.

"WELL!" Mary crowed. "I'm glad to see that every so often you break down and wear pants!"

Cord turned to see his cousin just closing the door that led from the cockpit into the companionway. He pinned her with a dark look. "Mary, I'm not in the mood."

Her biting laughter grated on his nerves. "Since when?"

He exhaled and turned away to finish buttoning his chambray shirt. "Can you make this quick? I've had a lot of bottom time today, and I'm—"

"Bottom time! *Ha!* Out of the mouths of rutting stags!"

He scowled darkly. "My mother—your mother's sister—taught me never to hit a woman, Mary, but she didn't mention anything about tossing them overboard."

Unbothered by his threat, Mary flounced down on the small couch and propped her legs on the miniature coffee table. "Get over here." She gestured pointedly toward the chair opposite her. "I'm mad and when I'm mad—"

"I know. When you're mad, you do your Morton Downey, Jr. routine." He ambled over to the chair and sat down. Lifting a booted foot to the coffee table, he swept her feet to the floor. "You have five minutes, Mort. Then I'm going to clean up for dinner."

She snorted at him and with a great flourish placed her feet on top of his boot. "Have you no scruples, seducing Tess under the very nose of her fiancé? Answer me that!"

Cord lifted his foot, toppling her again. He hunched forward, leaning on his knees to eye her through narrowed lashes. "I was not under the impression the lady was committed."

"Don't change the subject," she said shortly. "Answer my question. How could you seduce her under his nose?"

Cord didn't answer for a moment while he rested his chin on his fists. Finally his frown resolved itself into a thoughtful expression. "I hope she doesn't say yes to Nolan."

Mary's brows shot up in surprise. "Why do you hope that? What does it matter to you who she commits to?"

He lowered his gaze from hers. A shrug was his only answer.

"Do you want her?" She chuckled without humor. "Wrong question. Do you love her?"

Cord's eyes flew to meet Mary's challenging gaze and his frown returned. "I just don't think Nolan's right for her."

"Oh, I see. . . ." Mary's lips curled sarcastically. "Well, you have quite an ego if you think you can prove another man isn't right for a woman by taking her to *your* bed."

He leaned back tiredly in the chair. "I meant, Tess deserves better."

"Better?" Mary repeated, incredulous. "What's wrong with Nolan? Is he a woman beater or an escaped felon? How many people has he bludgeoned with his calculator? What exactly is wrong with him, Cord?"

"I don't know, just . . ." Cord couldn't put his feelings into words. He pushed himself up from the chair. Mary had made her point. He knew he'd been a jerk, and he didn't care to be lambasted about it any longer. "Your five minutes are up."

"Like fun they are." She jumped up, too, drawing his eyes. Aiming an accusing finger at his nose, she charged, "So, 'better' to you is a few steamy romps between the covers and a promise to write?" She rolled her eyes, pretending to swoon. "My hero!"

Her sarcasm did its work. He flinched.

"Don't you see how faulty your logic has become lately? What's the matter with you? You used to be such a smart kid."

"Look, Mary," Cord began, taking her hand. "Leave it alone, will you? It won't happen again."

She snorted. "Till when? After the eleven o'clock news?" Pulling her hand away from his, she warned, "Look, Cord, you can go around breaking as many hearts as you want, anywhere else, but since I booked this inn, I'd feel responsible if you broke that sweet woman's heart. I like her, even if you don't."

"Dammit to hell, Mary. I like her!"

"Well, pin a rose on you and call you Rosie!" She planted her fists on her hips. "I've seen how you *like* her and I'm not impressed." She brushed past him and was at the door when, apparently having second thoughts, she turned around, adding less curtly, "I've had my say. I love you, Cord." She sighed. "It's just that I'm getting weary of hearing sob stories from your cast-off women. Sometimes—" she averted her gaze, fiddling absently with the door-knob "—sometimes I wish you were pot-bellied and had a big wart on your nose. I'd sleep easier." The door banged shut at her back and she was gone.

Cord flashed a thwarted glance toward heaven. He shrugged his hands into his hip pockets, wishing Mary would stay out of his private affairs. To hell with whether she'd sleep easier or not. He wanted to sleep easier, too. He hadn't had two hours rest in the past two days, what with brooding about Tess, being angry with her, with himself, with Nolan and then being given the totally unexpected gift of making wild love to her all last night.

His half smile was bleak. He probably looked as rotten as he felt, warts or no warts. He climbed the steps to the deck to gather up his diving equipment and stow it, but even as he busied himself, dark thoughts nagged him.

Mary had told him nothing he hadn't told himself that morning. He'd already vowed that he was going to leave Tess alone. Let her live her own life, make her own choices. But something about the decision bothered him. He knew he was well out of it and that any decisions Tess made were none of his business. But somehow, that knowledge didn't sit easily with him. His life seemed a little off center, and there was a restless twisting in his gut. He didn't like it.

10

TESS HAD AVOIDED CORD that evening, keeping to her office. The one glimpse she'd had of him as he was going into the dining room for dinner had given her the distinct impression that her maneuverings were unnecessary. He'd been involved in a conversation with Quillan and Jewel, who'd had a hand on the arm of each of her escorts. Cord had been chuckling at one of Jewel's anecdotes as they'd passed Tess. He'd appeared oblivious to the fact that she was there at all.

That was fine. *Just fine.* She sat up abruptly in her bed, feeling anything but fine. Turning on her bedside lamp, she squinted at her alarm clock. It was one-thirty in the morning. She breathed a long sigh and reached for the pack of cigarettes she'd disgusted herself by buying on her way to bed. The pack was now half empty.

After lighting a cigarette, she blew a thin stream of smoke and settled back into her pillows. The dim circle of lamplight illuminated the ceiling, ornately decorated with a stucco oval, around which revolved semicircles of fans, and a faintly visible outer border of urns and swags.

She used to think hers was a most spectacular ceiling, but now she felt like a prisoner in a rococo jail. Lifting the cigarette to her lips, Tess realized her hand was trembling. Utterly unhappy, she felt a tear trail across her temple and slide into her ear.

After taking another drag, she propped herself up on one elbow and crushed the cigarette. She was being pathetic and maudlin. She smashed the cigarette to an unrecognizable pulp, deciding she'd allowed herself enough self-pity for one day. Life was what it was, and she had to make the best of her situation. That was simply that! She must get hold of herself, get back on track. Nolan was out of her life, and rightly so. Now she just had to get Cord Redigo out of her soul.

A loud pounding at her door scared the wits out of her. She had bounded from her bed and was standing barefoot, halfway to the door, before she realized she'd reacted at all. With her hand to her throat, she was about to cry out when she heard Kalvin's excited shout, "Ms Mankiller, we've seen 'im! We've seen *Champ!* Come a-runnin'!"

She had the light on now, and was yanking on her pink satin robe. "I'm coming. That's wonderful. . . ."

Before she could get anything else out, she heard Kalvin repeating his excited message at Cord's door. She gritted her teeth and shoved her feet into pink scuffs before scurrying out the door ahead of either her handyman or her nemesis. She didn't want to take the time to change and possibly miss seeing Champ, but neither did she relish the idea of confronting Cord in her nightgown.

She had gone down only one flight of stairs before Cord and Kalvin caught up with her. Cord had thrown on a pair of jeans, loafers without socks, and was pulling on a plaid shirt as he reached her. "Evening," he murmured as he and Kalvin passed her on the landing. "Be careful in those slippers."

She didn't respond. It wouldn't have done much good, anyway. He was long gone. So much for her crafty plan to avoid him. Obviously the little tumble in his bed last night was the sum and substance of everything he'd wanted from her.

"Thus ends the second and last chapter in my life containing Cord Redigo," she mumbled under her breath as she fled out of the kitchen and toward the reception hall. She struggled for a minute with the patio door, which insisted on sticking. She cursed it for several seconds before she finally jiggled it open and dashed across the patio and through the garden to the cliff where several tousled, groggy cryptozoologists had gathered. She squinted to take in the scene in the scanty moonlight.

Mary was in a terry robe, hopping around with one foot bare and one sheathed in a fuzzy slipper, her hair a comedy of pincurls. Kalvin was pointing excitedly into the mist that hugged the lake's surface. The Inch sisters were engaged in a giggling fit that bordered on hysteria.

Tess tugged her robe around her, realizing the night air was a bit cool for her attire. When she reached the cliff's edge, she could see Cord focusing a binocular-type device over the lake.

"What's that thing?" she asked aloud, and then clamped her mouth shut. She hadn't intended to engage him in direct conversation.

"Night-vision scope," he murmured as he lowered it and handed it back to Ella Inch. "Take a look," he told her, a small smile curving his lips.

"Champ?" Tess asked, unable to help herself.

"You'll see it in a minute. It's coming toward shore."

"Oh, my Lord. Is it?" she squeaked, peering into the semidarkness. There was a half moon, but the low mist kissing the surface of the lake obscured what miserly vision they had. "How can you be so calm, Cord? Anybody have a camera?" she cried.

"I do," Kalvin chimed in. "I remembered this time."

As Kalvin aimed his camera and the rest of the hushed group stared at the lake awaiting the wondrous first glimpse of Lake Champlain's famous monster, Cord turned to go.

Tess glanced his way, startled to realize that he was leaving. Movement near the shore caught her eye as a stag with a magnificent rack of antlers scrambled from the water and loped along the rocks for about ten yards before clambering up the slope and disappearing into a stand of spruce.

"It was a deer," cried Etta and Ella Inch in unison.

"Damn, damn, damn, *damn!*" Mary stomped around, throwing her hands up in the air. *"Damn, damn, damn . . ."* She turned back to the night surveillance team that consisted of Etta, Ella and Kalvin. Working at a limp smile of encouragement, she said, "Don't be disheartened, you're doing a fine job. Keep up the vigilant work." Then with a little limp-hop she turned away, muttering several more damns as she bobbed back toward the inn.

Tess stood there for a minute until Kalvin, Etta and Ella had resumed their watch positions, pads and pencils in hand, night scopes at the ready.

After a moment, a shiver rushed up her spine, making her teeth chatter. She was chilled through. Turning back toward the darkened inn, she realized with some surprise that everyone else was gone.

She quickened her step, not wanting to catch cold. Glancing down to watch her step along the garden path, she noticed that her nipples were pressing against the lacy bodice of her robe. "Well," she muttered as she shuffled hurriedly across the patio, "At least I won't have to face Cord this way."

"Did you say something to me?"

Tess's head shot up to see Cord opening the patio door for her. "Uh, no." Feeling dishevelled and half naked, she brushed by him, crossing her arms over her chest. "Thanks. Uh . . . I thought you'd gone to bed."

"Mary and I were talking. When I saw you coming, I thought you might need a hand with this door. It sticks."

"I know it sticks," she retorted, ill at ease being so near to him. "I'm the one who told you it sticks."

"Right. I'd forgotten." He eyed her searchingly, and she armed herself for another bout of frustration.

The pause was awkward.

Her hungry eyes devoured him against her will, noting the way the dim light fell on the craggy angles and planes of his face. Her heart began to thud with alarm over her unwise attraction to him. Needing to get away quickly, she shot him a terse, "Well, good ni—"

"Was that Champ sighting illuminating for you?" he said, interrupting her.

She peered sideways at him. "Don't gloat."

"I'm not."

"You loved it," she threw back. "I saw you smile."

"It was kind of funny," he told her honestly. "But you're wrong, you know. Discovering a Champ-type creature would be an unequaled thrill—it's just not very likely."

"I think this is where I came in." She avoided his eyes as she moved past him. "I'm going to bed."

She breezed away from him, heading toward the hallway that led to the kitchen. He said nothing to halt her; didn't call her back and she heard no footsteps to indicate that he was following. There was no reason for him to do any of those things, she knew. But loving him the way she did made it very hard to walk away. Thwarted, heartsick and feeling lost, she cast her gaze down at the wood-planked floor.

Unaccountably her footsteps slowed until she was no longer moving. Then, surprising her as much as anything she'd ever done, she turned back to face him, her stance shy and reluctant.

He was still where she'd left him, though he'd half turned away. When he heard her turn, he shifted his gaze.

His glance briefly touched her body, stealing her breath, before settling on her face. Emotions she couldn't interpret played across his clean features. His mouth was turned down at the corners as he frowned, and there was an endearing perplexity in his eyes as he waited for her to speak her piece.

She swallowed. Clasping her hands together tightly, she blurted out, "Nolan and I won't be seeing each other anymore. We've decided not to get married." Though she hated to talk about something so personal, she felt compelled to do so. After all, Cord had been the one to point out a very important flaw in her relationship with Nolan. He had been right, and she thought he deserved to be told, even if she had to endure an I-told-you-so smirk.

Deep down, she had another reason for telling him, a dear but farfetched dream. Maybe—just maybe—Cord would be glad about it. Maybe he'd run to her, swing her up into his arms and tell her that was what he'd been hoping to hear—that he loved her, wanted her to marry him. Unable to breathe, she waited for his reaction.

Cord's eyes had narrowed assessingly. He stared at her for a long moment before finally shaking his head with regret. *"Hell,"* he rasped, dragging a hand through his hair.

Tess watched him, stung with disbelief. She hadn't expected anger. Feeling suddenly sick, she hugged herself.

"I was an ass to interfere," he growled, making her jump. "I should have kept out of your business. I'm sorry."

His eyes were vivid, ironically beautiful, glistening with self-loathing. That unhappy look hurt Tess more than any words could have.

He was *sorry*! Sorry that it had been his "interference" that had been her sole cause for ending her affair with Nolan. Cord's lovemaking had made her realize she couldn't marry another man as long as Cord could take her in his arms and make her feel so alive, so complete. And now that he'd ruined her for any other man, he was sorry?

Her insides contracted in shame and fury. Trying to salvage a thread of her pride, she threw a glare at him and snapped, "Don't beat yourself up about it. I couldn't have loved Nolan if I was so easily side-tracked by *you*!"

She knew her remark was mean-spirited, but she was too torn apart to guard her tongue. The man she loved—had always loved—was sorry she wasn't marrying someone else! She swallowed down the nausea swimming in her throat.

Hurt flamed in his eyes, but she forced herself to be invulnerable to that look.

The shrill ringing of the office phone broke the sharp silence like a bullet splintering glass. Her body was so stabbed through with tension that she had to stifle an urge to scream.

She mumbled something unintelligible and rushed behind the counter to answer the wall phone. When she lifted the receiver, her hand shook, and she fumbled with it for several seconds before she could get it to her ear. "Lost Cove Inn." Her voice sounded small, her words faltering. "May I . . . help you?"

The German-accented voice on the other end was indistinct beneath static, but she could make out that the man wanted to speak to Cord. She turned to look at him. He was facing her, his feet slightly apart as he watched her, his features grave.

Her heart thudded heavily beneath her weightless satin wrap, and she reached for the support of the registration desk as she said, "Just a moment, please."

She held the receiver toward him in a lethargic hand. "For you . . ."

Feeling a strong sense of foreboding, she sagged against the reception desk as he crossed the distance to her.

"Hello?"

She felt the warmth of his body beside her and found it hard to breathe. Feeling awkward and weak, she brushed a wayward strand of hair away from her cheek.

"Just an hour ago?" Cord asked quietly. "I'm honored, Hans. Tell Dr. Ellerby I'll be there as soon as possible."

When he'd hung up the receiver, Tess's brows gathered in a dark storm. He was leaving, going somewhere very far away. She cringed at the thought. Reluctantly, she met his gaze.

"You're going away," she breathed. It wasn't a question.

He nodded and her heart crashed to the leather soles of her slippers. All the anger and resentment drained out of her and she sagged with defeat. Cord was walking out of her life again. This time it was forever. Deep down, she had known this moment would come, but now that it was here, she was devastated.

"That was my partner. There's been a stranding of a megamouth shark on the coast of Australia. It's a new species, first discovered in 1976. There've only been three specimens found to date." He finished solemnly, "It's alive. The chance to observe one is a rare privilege."

"Will you be back?"

"I doubt it," he said, his mouth thinning. "I need to get to Grande Comore and relieve Hans." His somber expression said far more than his words. He was telling her goodbye, that it was for the best that he exit her life cleanly and quickly—like the surgical severing of a body part.

The pain his quiet words had inflicted made him blur before her, and she averted her gaze so that he couldn't see the telltale glisten in her eyes. "I see," she murmured. "Well, good luck with your life. . . ."

"Thank you, Tessa Jane."

Surreptitiously wiping her eyes, she turned back to look at him.

Knitting his brows, he said, "I'd better go pack."

As a cover for her growing despair, she adopted a lofty tone. "In the morning, I'll tell Mary where you've gone."

"No need. I'll drop by her room before I leave." He looked ill at ease. "Would you mind calling a taxi?"

Tess nodded listlessly.

He could see the forlorn look in her features, the awful vulnerability. Her perfume drifted around him, a delicate fragrance reminiscent of lily of the valley, reminiscent, too, of the loving they'd shared. Her striking ebony hair made a dark frame around her exotic face, and her green eyes swam with bright sadness. She was beautiful. Inside and out. Beautiful enough for any man—leggy blondes be damned. But there was no room in his life for a woman, not a permanent one, anyway. Somehow, right now, that seemed like a damned shame.

He hadn't meant to touch her, but his hands seemed to take on a life of their own, reaching out to caress her fevered cheeks. "Take care of yourself, Tessa Jane," he whispered. His fingertips lingered for a moment on her skin, and he stared at her wordlessly, considering saying more. Thinking better of it, he stepped back.

Vowing not to reveal how much his touch unsettled her, she lifted her chin. "Goodbye, Cord."

He watched her for a moment, and then, without another word, he turned away.

He didn't even say goodbye, Tess thought, twisting around to lean heavily on the polished reception desk. When she'd gathered the strength to look up, she could do nothing but stare helplessly as the tall, self-possessed man she loved walked out of her life.

EIGHT DAYS AFTER Cord's abrupt departure, two important events occurred. First, Tess's aunt Jewel pulled her aside and told her that she and Quillan were planning to be married. The second bit of news was equally dramatic, but less welcome. Tess had opened her latest issue of the *Smithsonian* magazine and had seen, to her dismay, picture after picture of Cord Redigo and his bearded German partner, Hans Gruber, involved in capturing and stabilizing the two live coelacanths Cord had brought to New York earlier that month.

His crooked smile tormented her from the glossy pages. There were pictures of Cord, naked to the waist, his sun-bronzed torso glistening with sea spray. There were spectacular color photos of Cord and Hans in their submersible. And Cord, his expression serious, yet looking vigorous and trim, was pictured as he oversaw the loading of the tank and its water cooling system aboard a U.S. Army transport plane.

Tess flipped a page irritably and was forced to stare again into Cord's face, fresh and smiling, as he arrived in New York; and finally, tall and elegant in a tuxedo, being greeted by New York's scientific and political notables.

She'd groaned, slammed the magazine shut and thrown it on her desk. "What was the story about, anyway—fish or Cord Redigo?" she snapped, stalking from her office. "The photographer had to have been a woman!"

She'd been consumed by a gnawing restlessness since the night Cord had walked away. She despised herself for allowing him to rule her emotions even half a world away. She also hated herself for not being able to be appropriately delighted by Jewel and Quillan's approaching wedding. Damn Cord, anyway!

ON THE SECOND-WEEK anniversary of Cord's absence, Tess and Mary gave a surprise engagement party for Jewel and Quillan. Quillan's daughter, Myra Quimby-Park, Natalie's mother, had come up from Burlington to attend. Tess liked the talkative redhead and threw herself into making a new friend. She'd introduced Myra, a single parent, to Nolan, who had also been invited to the party. Tess noticed with interest that they'd hit it off immediately. By the end of the party, it looked as if Nolan was a man whose broken heart was on the mend.

Love seemed to be running rampant at Lost Cove Inn of late, Tess observed, though Cupid had dismal aim when it came to her. Nevertheless she was happy for Jewel and Quillan, and for what appeared to be brewing with Nolan and Myra.

She looked at her watch. It was nearly two in the morning. The party had been over for an hour. The place had been cleaned and polished and all the help was gone. Though she was bone weary, Tess didn't want to sleep, didn't want to be bedeviled by her dreams.

She decided to make a last swing around the inn to check things out before heading to her lonely bed. Glancing into her office, she saw the *Smithsonian* on her desk and hesitated only a minute before going and snatching it up.

Tucking it under her arm, she headed into the kitchen, but before she started for the stairs, she stuffed the magazine into the trash compactor. With a vengeance, she switched on the machine then hurried toward the staircase muttering, "So much for Dr. Cord Redigo."

When she reached the first landing and the noisy machine had fallen quiet, she was clutched by a choking feeling of absolute misery. She could crush all the *Smithsonian* magazines in the world, and it wouldn't change the simple fact that Cord had walked away. A cry welled up in her throat. Fleeing up the darkened stairway, she swiped away a preposterous tear.

11

THE WEATHER WAS RAINY AND FOGGY, making lake observation poor. It was the last day of June, and also the last day of the cryptozoologists' stay at Lost Cove Inn. Tess was checking with Sugar to make sure everything was running smoothly in preparation for the farewell dinner, but her heart wasn't in it.

"Okay, that's everything," she said, and then added, "Have the kitchen help start setting the tables a little before six."

"Gotcha, boss." Sugar saluted, and swiveled around to face the counter where she'd been snapping green beans. Humming off key, she returned to her own little world behind her earphones.

Tess pushed through the kitchen door into the dining room and almost ran headlong into Mary. "Oh—" she exhaled her relief at avoiding a collision "—hello."

Mary stepped back and smoothed her short hair. It was an unnecessary, nervous gesture. "Hi, Tess." She smiled shyly. She'd been giving Tess that same painful, apologetic look ever since that terrible morning she'd caught Tess in Cord's bed.

Tess stifled a sigh and tried to look unbothered. 'How are you, Mary? Haven't seen you much today."

The older woman shrugged. "Well, you know. Last day and all. Doing a lot of packing up."

Tess nodded, feeling a tinge of regret. She'd grown to like the cryptozoologists. She was truly sorry they'd be going away with nothing to show for their efforts.

Mary seemed to sense Tess's thoughts and assured her hurriedly, "Did I tell you about the erratic markings on the paper chart recorder, yesterday? And that last week we had odd shadows on our underwater film?"

Tess shook her head, confused.

"Well, we all agree that the markings merit further study. And with sophisticated enhancement, the film could be very revealing."

"Oh?" Tess smiled, feeling a little better. "I'm glad, Mary. Let me know, will you?"

She put a friendly hand on Tess's arm. "I will. Let's do keep in touch."

Tess looked down, unable to speak. She didn't think it would be wise to keep in touch with Cord's cousin. But how did she tell Mary?

"You really need to develop a poker face, kid. I can read every thought in that pretty, sad face." Mary squeezed Tess's arm. "Look, I love Cord, but I know he has gigantic faults. He's a scoundrel where women are concerned. He works too hard for his own good, and he's a little too crazy about fish for my taste. You're lucky to be rid of him."

Tess forced a grin in spite of her mood. She offered quietly, "Sure. We'll keep in touch, if you'd like."

Mary hiked a thin brow. "Okay. We won't talk about him." She patted Tess's elbow. "Gotta go for now. Etta and Ella want me to help pick their music for tonight's show." She grimaced. "I hope they know a really fast version of the Minute Waltz."

Tess laughed. "If they do, it's sure to be a polka."

"Oh, agony!" Mary rolled her eyes, then added, "Are you going to recite any poetry?"

"Speaking of agony?" Tess kidded.

"I didn't mean it like that," Mary countered, but her cheeks colored, giving away her true feelings about Tess's marginal talents.

Tess silently agreed, but said only, "Not tonight. It's your party. I'm simply going to play innkeeper and stay out of the limelight."

"Oh, well . . ." Mary appeared uncharacteristically flustered. "Tess, it's been a grand month, really." She held out her hand. "We'll surely come back next year, if it's okay with you."

Accepting Mary's hand, Tess said, "I'll look forward to it." But in her heart the idea of having her life drag on for another year, unchanged, seemed a dismal sentence.

Mary's handshake was brief, and seconds later she was gone, leaving Tess alone. She cast a distracted gaze out the bank of arched windows that faced the lake. The sky was gray, growing even more gloomy with the approaching dusk.

When three of the young kitchen helpers burst through the swinging door, giggling and chattering as they began to place cutlery, napkins and vases containing small bouquets of daisies on the long tables, Tess decided she needed to get away, to be alone.

SHE FIDGETED on the rocky ledge for a solid hour before she decided she had to move. She wanted to run, but it was dark and there was no place to go. With the moon peeping timidly from behind low clouds, she headed down the steep wooden staircase toward the rocky shore, her footsteps sounding heavy and hollow to her ears. About ten feet from the bottom, she became engulfed in the somber fog that blanketed the lake's surface.

The setting was perfect for her mood. She strolled idly along the shoreline, wrapped in a cocoon of oblivion. From far away, she could hear the strains of an accordion-piano duet and realized the cryptozoologists' party was in full swing.

Listening intently for a moment, she recognized the tune as "Auld Lang Syne," and shook her head. It was the most peppy version of the song she'd ever heard, or perhaps "crazed" was more appropriate. Her lips quirked in a reluctant grin.

She kicked a stone and listened as it clattered across other rocks and then plunked into the deep cove several yards away. Turning, she faced the invisible lake and choked down a harsh breath. She jammed her hands into the deep pockets of her white, flared skirt, and allowed herself to succumb to her defeat.

She was to blame for all her troubles. It had been she who had gone to him—given herself to him—on that hayride so long ago.

It had been she who, once again, had initiated the lovemaking on the cabin cruiser, and it had also been she who had gone to his room that night—their only night together.

She had always been the one flustered, out of sorts and off balance while he had remained cool, elegant and in control. That was certainly not the image of a man head over heels in love. She'd been an idiot to ever dream of such a thing.

Cord had never chased her, never fed her any lines of undying love. He'd never lied or led her on. So if she had anyone to blame for her unhappiness, it wasn't Cord Redigo.

She supposed he had taken advantage of her willingness, but if that was a crime, then every adult male on earth who'd ever made love to a dewy-eyed female would be in prison!

Maybe the fact that she would never see Cord again would teach her a lesson—a lesson about rashness—and make her more circumspect in future relationships with men. But even as she was rationalizing a possible value of The Cord Redigo Lesson, she knew it was a fool's errand. She was, had always been and would always be, just short of prudish in her dealings with men... with the singular exception of Cord Redigo.

She knew in her heart that this was a tragic loss to her life, a loss no wisdom could be gleaned from. She could only attempt to go on, hope for the best and try *never* to look back.

With tears blurring her vision, she searched the secretive fog for answers she knew were not there. Needing to talk to someone, to at least voice her unhappiness, she threw out a question to the mythical monster she chose to believe in. "Is the kind of love I want as elusive as you are, Champ?" she cried softly, her voice a hushed plea.

The silence that followed hung about her as heavily as the fog, and she shivered both with cold and desolation. Her turtleneck sweater didn't seem to be keeping out the damp any better than her heart was fighting off her despair.

"Maybe what you're looking for isn't so elusive," a disembodied voice suggested, making her twist back suddenly, her eyes widening with shock.

"Could you feel secure and free on the island of Grande Comore?"

Though the initial shock was wearing off, her heart still hammered with disbelief as she squinted vainly to see through the curtain of mist.

With a hand at her throat, she began to discern a ghostly vision through the undulating fingers of haze, a lean specter sauntering in her direction. Though the voice was familiar and the elegant gait made her thrill with recollection, she didn't dare believe it could really be Cord. She told herself it was an hallucination, brought on because her need for him was so great, her mind so clouded by lack of sleep...that was all it was. She closed her eyes to blink away the apparition. When she opened them again, he was very near.

"Tessa Jane?" he asked gravely. "Did you hear me?"

She clutched her hands together, her voice a thin thread as she breathed, "Is it really you?"

"Me and about twenty-four hours of flying."

When she'd collected herself enough to notice how rumpled and tired he looked, she frowned with worry. His eyes were rimmed with blue shadows. His crooked mouth, darkened with a day's growth of beard, was lifted only slightly in a smile, as though he was uncertain of his welcome. His platinum-streaked hair was mussed, crying out to be smoothed by loving hands.

She swallowed, her eyes roaming desperately over him. His silver-blue silk slacks were badly wrinkled. The white button-down shirt was equally disheveled and open at the collar. A striped tie was loosened and askew; the matching suitcoat sported several rust-colored splotches.

"You don't look so good," she observed gently.

He chuckled and then grew serious. "You do. You're the best damned sight I've seen in two weeks."

She stared. Unable to accept the truth of his words, she asked, "What happened to you?"

He shrugged. "Skipping the gory details, I'll put it this way. Have you ever made a decision and then run from one end of Sydney's international airport to another?"

She shook her head, befuddled.

"Well, don't. It can't be done, unless you're a crazy man."

He chuckled ruefully. "That was just the beginning. There weren't any seats on the Denver-to-Chicago leg, so I paid a woman a hundred bucks to let me hold her two-year-old on my lap so I could get on the flight. Somewhere over the Rockies little Jennifer Armstrong upchucked chocolate pudding all over my coat. But it was worth it, because now I'm here."

"What are you saying?" Tess asked, not even hoping that he'd come back because of her. She was so numb and confused.

He reached out, his hard, tanned fingers lacing through her trembling ones. "I'm saying I love you, Tessa Jane. I'm saying that since I left you, I've realized there's more to life than work. I'm saying that I've been looking for something more. . . ."

Concern shadowed his features and then he smiled at her. "That something was you."

His revelation left her speechless and weak.

"I want you to marry me," he said, stroking her hair back from her face. "I don't want to go back to Grande Comore without you." His glance held quick concern. "Could you be secure roaming the face of the earth with me?"

A wave of pure happiness rushed over her. "Oh, Cord—" She choked back a sob. A hut on a remote island sounded like a wonderful place to be . . . or a hotel in Paris . . . or even an inflatable rubber dinghy during a rainstorm, as long as Cord was beside her. "Are you sure?" she asked, her lips trembling.

"I've never been so sure about anything, darling." He dipped his head, blotting out a brief shaft of moonlight that had penetrated their delicious privacy. His mouth caught hers with a longing she had never known. "Never been so sure . . ." he repeated hoarsely against her lips.

She caught her breath as his arms bound her to him. Their kiss was deep and lingering, and when Cord finally drew away, she could hear his rasping breath in her ear. "You haven't answered me, you know."

Feeling light-headed, she pressed him ever so slightly away and looked into his face. His eyes blazed with unbridled desire.

"Do you really think I haven't answered you?"

"I want to hear it," he confessed softly.

She could only stare at the raw vulnerability etched over his lean features.

"I missed you while I was gone." He took a deep breath. "Could hardly think about my work." He kissed her again, full on the mouth, searing her to her core. "I was desperate to make you disappear from my thoughts, but nothing worked."

She smiled up at him with unrestrained joy. "So you think marriage might cure you?"

His smile was tentative, his eyes heated, yet soft. "Is that a yes or a no?"

After a pause during which she tried to form the words to tell him that she had always loved him, he asked, "What if I promise I'll try not to need you, except to love me back?"

She swallowed, working to dislodge her heart, which had just flown to her throat.

"Tessa Jane," he pleaded through a groan. "Say something."

At long last, after all the years and all the tears, Cord Redigo actually loved her. "Do I have to quit smoking?" she said, not believing her own ears—what a dumb thing to say! But, Cord was grinning at her and that was all that mattered.

He shook his head. "Don't change a thing for me. I'm crazy about hacking coughs."

The love in his eyes took her breath away. The time for teasing was over. "Oh, Cord . . ." she sighed. "Do you know how long I've loved you?"

His expression grew somber and he hugged her to him. "About as long as I've loved you," he murmured, his voice rough with emotion. "I realize now why I've avoided virgins all these years. You never get over them."

An odd sound from the direction of the cove drew their attention and they turned toward it, though they remained entwined in an embrace.

"What was that?" Tess whispered, looking up at Cord.

He shook his head, listening. "I don't know. Sounded like something came up out of the water. Something big."

Tess squinted into the mist. "Can you see anything?"

"Nothing."

"Cord..." She chewed on the inside of her cheek for a moment before she ventured, "Do you have the feeling we're being watched?"

"Yeah." He nodded and turned to face her. When their eyes met, they both had the same crazy thought and shared a smile.

"No . . ." Cord denied with a shake of his tawny head. "It can't be."

She raised a brow.

"Okay. . ." He hugged her to him. "With you in my arms, I can believe anything. Even that our marriage is being blessed by a shy monster." With that, he swept her up in his arms, chuckling. "Baby, you've affected my mind."

Light laughter gurgled in her throat. Nuzzling his neck she promised, "If you can admit to maybe believing in Champ, I guess I can quit smoking. Do you think you could develop an affection for me without the hacking cough?"

"I could try," he teased, "and I plan to, just as soon as I get cleaned up."

"Maybe I could help." She unbuttoned the top button on his shirt and boldly ran her hand over his furred chest. "I'm very good with soap."

"Oh, lady, you're on." He hiked her up to a better position in his arms. "But first, I want to know if you're going to marry me or if you're just toying with my affections."

"Okay, okay." She draped an arm across his shoulders, pretending nonchalance. "I'll marry you."

"That wasn't very romantic." There was a charming pout in his voice.

"It wasn't? Oh. Sorry." With impish delight she dipped her tongue in his ear.

"That's better . . ." He groaned. "Whoa, Tessa Jane, I won't be able to walk if you—Tess—I'm going to pay you back for this."

"Please do . . ." she urged, and with a melodic sigh, settled her head on his shoulder.

They grew quiet, content with the aura of their love. Cord carried her toward the dock where the cabin cruiser was tied up.

"Did I tell you that Quillan and Jewel are getting married?" she asked after a minute.

"No." Cord chuckled. "Maybe we can make it a double ceremony."

"And did I tell you that Nolan invited Quillan's daughter, Myra, to the annual CPA Man of the Year Dinner? I think Nolan's going to win it. Myra's a nice woman. . . ."

"Witty and spontaneous, I hope."

Tess looked up at him, puzzled. Then she smiled, understanding his point. "Yes—witty and spontaneous enough for Nolan's needs, anyway. She's been frantically searching for a job since the restaurant she managed got bought out."

"There's going to be a 'frantic' job opening at a certain inn very soon," he reminded her.

"You know?" Tess kissed his throat. "I think she'd be perfect."

"I'd hire her, fast, if I were you." He mounted the dock and with broad strides headed toward the cruiser. "On second thought, tomorrow morning will do."

"My thinking exactly." Tess smiled up at him, a sensuous promise in her eyes.

Suddenly, they both tensed, growing alert. They sensed that something hiding in the fog had just slipped beneath the surface of Lake Champlain.

"So long, Champ," Tess murmured as Cord helped her aboard the cruiser.

"What?" he asked.

Feeling silly and worrying that Cord would think her hopelessly sentimental, she told him something that was true, even though she hadn't just voiced it. "I said, 'I love you.'"

As he draped a protective arm about her, the devoted gleam in his eyes took her breath away, and she stood motionless, lost in the beauty of those clear blue eyes.

"That's what I thought you said." He bent to brush the top of her head with a kiss, murmuring against her hair, "You might tell him we'll see him next summer."

She laughed and hugged his middle. "I think he knows."

"What else do you think?" he asked, leading her toward the cabin door.

"I think I'm going to like Grande Comore."

"Why do you think that?"

"I read somewhere that the equatorial night skies are sequined with shooting stars so clear that they trail comets' tails behind them. Is that true?"

"Uh-huh." His chuckle was rich and sexy. "And Grande Comore also has the world's largest active volcanic crater. That's why I live offshore on my cruiser."

"Sounds divine," she sighed dreamily.

"You'd be living on a boat, on water, beneath a volcano. Not very secure."

"I'll love it," she assured him.

"Over your fear of water completely?"

"What fear of water?" She sighed. "I love water. Water brought you back to me—at least something *in* water."

"Champ, or my coelacanths?"

"Does it matter?"

"You're right." He touched her chin, drawing her gaze. His smile was the sweetest, gentlest sight she'd ever seen. He whispered, "Well, Miss-Unafraid-Bathing-Beauty, did I tell you that Grande Comore has some nice beaches?"

"Good." Feeling absolutely wonderful, she inhaled the damp crispness of the night air mingled with Cord's warm, sultry scent. "I'd hate to be stuck on some remote island paradise with you *without* nice beaches."

"You're a sassy woman."

"You don't like sassy women?" She peered up at him from beneath her lashes.

"You know exactly what I like," he growled, nipping the lobe of her ear.

She struggled for breath as his teeth worked their erotic magic. "I've heard you're crazy about fish."

With a hearty laugh, he led her through the cabin door. His hungry mouth found her throat as he unzipped the back of her sweater then trailed hot kisses down her newly exposed flesh, nipping and licking as he vowed lustily, "I've never done this to a fish. . . ." His hands roamed, enticing and titillating. "Or this. . ."

"Oh . . . Cord . . . oh . . ." she whimpered, quivering with delight. He loved her, and as sure as there was breath in her body, he would prove that to her again and again tonight. And for all their nights to come.

The door to the companionway closed at their backs, and a gentle breeze began to blow away the shroud of fog. It promised to be a bright, beautiful morning. But before that new day dawned, the night on Lake Champlain would be as white-hot and incendiary as any volcanic eruption Grande Comore could boast. For on this night, Tessa Jane Mankiller would know a wild, sweet rebirth.

She would begin to spread her wings, to fly free at last, like one of her silken kites. With Cord's devotion as her only anchor, she would come to know that "security" and "freedom" are myths, but for the sanctuary of true, unselfish love.

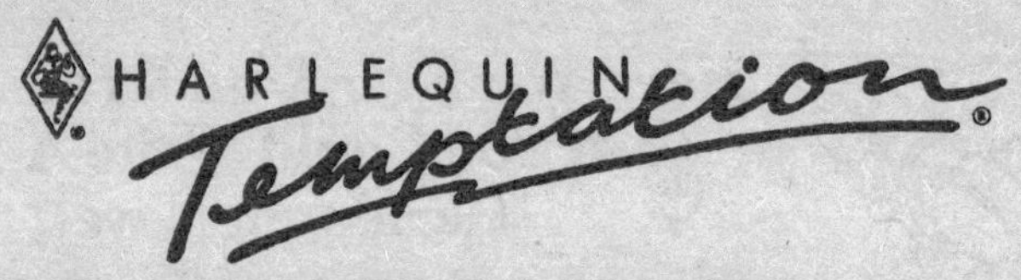

COMING NEXT MONTH

#281 I DO, AGAIN Carin Rafferty

Lust at first sight led to a hasty marriage for Sirena and Noah and, ultimately, to an even hastier divorce. Or so they thought.... Two years later the awful truth emerged—the marriage was still intact . . . and so was the lust!

#282 TOO MANY HUSBANDS Elise Title

All Casey Croyden wanted for Christmas was a husband. Not a permanent one—just a man to play the part and help her impress the traditional Japanese businessman she was entertaining over the holidays. Sounded simple enough—hire one from Actors Equity. But when John Gallagher arrived on her doorstep the attraction between them was no act!

#283 COULD IT BE MAGIC Gina Wilkins

Schoolteacher Gwen DeClerk was stable and reliable—a perfect foil for international celebrity Jeremy Kane's offbeat, driven personality. And that was why he was attracted to her. But there was a side to Gwen he had yet to discover. Miss Prim and Proper was about to become Ms Hot and Heavy!

#284 WILDCAT Candace Schuler

It took the death of her grandfather to bring Stacey back to Texas, but this time she was determined to stay. Eleven years in Paris had transformed her from a wildcat into a woman to be reckoned with—and not even Ben Oakes was going to come between her and her birthright!

INDULGE A LITTLE SWEEPSTAKES

OFFICIAL RULES

SWEEPSTAKES RULES AND REGULATIONS. NO PURCHASE NECESSARY.

1. NO PURCHASE NECESSARY. To enter complete the official entry form and return with the invoice in the envelope provided. Or you may enter by printing your name, complete address and your daytime phone number on a 3 x 5 piece of paper. Include with your entry the hand printed words "Indulge A Little Sweepstakes." Mail your entry to: Indulge A Little Sweepstakes, P.O. Box 1397, Buffalo, NY 14269-1397. No mechanically reproduced entries accepted. Not responsible for late, lost, misdirected mail, or printing errors.

2. Three winners, one per month (Sept. 30, 1989, October 31, 1989 and November 30, 1989), will be selected in random drawings. All entries received prior to the drawing date will be eligible for that month's prize. This sweepstakes is under the supervision of MARDEN-KANE, INC. an independent judging organization whose decisions are final and binding. Winners will be notified by telephone and may be required to execute an affidavit of eligibility and release which must be returned within 14 days, or an alternate winner will be selected.

3. Prizes: 1st Grand Prize (1) a trip for two to Disneyworld in Orlando, Florida. Trip includes round trip air transportation, hotel accommodations for seven days and six nights, plus up to $700 expense money (ARV $3,500). 2nd Grand Prize (1) a seven-night Chandris Caribbean Cruise for two includes transportation from nearest major airport, accommodations, meals plus up to $1,000 in expense money (ARV $4,300). 3rd Grand Prize (1) a ten-day Hawaiian holiday for two includes round trip air transportation for two, hotel accommodations, sightseeing, plus up to $1,200 in spending money (ARV $7,700). All trips subject to availability and must be taken as outlined on the entry form.

4. Sweepstakes open to residents of the U.S. and Canada 18 years or older except employees and the families of Torstar Corp., its affiliates, subsidiaries and Marden-Kane, Inc. and all other agencies and persons connected with conducting this sweepstakes. All Federal, State and local laws and regulations apply. Void wherever prohibited or restricted by law. Taxes, if any are the sole responsibility of the prize winners. Canadian winners will be required to answer a skill testing question. Winners consent to the use of their name, photograph and/or likeness for publicity purposes without additional compensation.

5. For a list of prize winners, send a stamped, self-addressed envelope to Indulge A Little Sweepstakes Winners, P.O. Box 701, Sayreville, NJ 08871.

DL-SWPS

INDULGE A LITTLE SWEEPSTAKES

OFFICIAL RULES

SWEEPSTAKES RULES AND REGULATIONS. NO PURCHASE NECESSARY.

1. NO PURCHASE NECESSARY. To enter complete the official entry form and return with the invoice in the envelope provided. Or you may enter by printing your name, complete address and your daytime phone number on a 3 x 5 piece of paper. Include with your entry the hand printed words "Indulge A Little Sweepstakes." Mail your entry to: Indulge A Little Sweepstakes, P.O. Box 1397, Buffalo, NY 14269-1397. No mechanically reproduced entries accepted. Not responsible for late, lost, misdirected mail, or printing errors.

2. Three winners, one per month (Sept. 30, 1989, October 31, 1989 and November 30, 1989), will be selected in random drawings. All entries received prior to the drawing date will be eligible for that month's prize. This sweepstakes is under the supervision of MARDEN-KANE, INC. an independent judging organization whose decisions are final and binding. Winners will be notified by telephone and may be required to execute an affidavit of eligibility and release which must be returned within 14 days, or an alternate winner will be selected.

3. Prizes: 1st Grand Prize (1) a trip for two to Disneyworld in Orlando, Florida. Trip includes round trip air transportation, hotel accommodations for seven days and six nights, plus up to $700 expense money (ARV $3,500). 2nd Grand Prize (1) a seven-night Chandris Caribbean Cruise for two includes transportation from nearest major airport, accommodations, meals plus up to $1,000 in expense money (ARV $4,300). 3rd Grand Prize (1) a ten-day Hawaiian holiday for two includes round trip air transportation for two, hotel accommodations, sightseeing, plus up to $1,200 in spending money (ARV $7,700). All trips subject to availability and must be taken as outlined on the entry form.

4. Sweepstakes open to residents of the U.S. and Canada 18 years or older except employees and the families of Torstar Corp., its affiliates, subsidiaries and Marden-Kane, Inc. and all other agencies and persons connected with conducting this sweepstakes. All Federal, State and local laws and regulations apply. Void wherever prohibited or restricted by law. Taxes, if any are the sole responsibility of the prize winners. Canadian winners will be required to answer a skill testing question. Winners consent to the use of their name, photograph and/or likeness for publicity purposes without additional compensation.

5. For a list of prize winners, send a stamped, self-addressed envelope to Indulge A Little Sweepstakes Winners, P.O. Box 701, Sayreville, NJ 08871.

© 1989 HARLEQUIN ENTERPRISES LTD.

DL-SWPS

INDULGE A LITTLE—WIN A LOT!

Summer of '89 Subscribers-Only Sweepstakes

OFFICIAL ENTRY FORM

This entry must be received by: Nov. 30, 1989
This month's winner will be notified by: Dec. 7, 1989
Trip must be taken between: Jan. 7, 1990–Jan. 7, 1991

YES, I want to win the 3-Island Hawaiian vacation for two! I understand the prize includes round-trip airfare, first-class hotels, and a daily allowance as revealed on the "Wallet" scratch-off card.

Name________________________________

Address______________________________

City__________ State/Prov.______ Zip/Postal Code______

Daytime phone number____________________
Area code

Return entries with invoice in envelope provided. Each book in this shipment has two entry coupons—and the more coupons you enter, the better your chances of winning!

DINDL-3

INDULGE A LITTLE—WIN A LOT!

Summer of '89 Subscribers-Only Sweepstakes

OFFICIAL ENTRY FORM

This entry must be received by: Nov. 30, 1989
This month's winner will be notified by: Dec. 7, 1989
Trip must be taken between: Jan. 7, 1990–Jan. 7, 1991

YES, I want to win the 3-Island Hawaiian vacation for two! I understand the prize includes round-trip airfare, first-class hotels, and a daily allowance as revealed on the "Wallet" scratch-off card.

Name________________________________

Address______________________________

City__________ State/Prov.______ Zip/Postal Code______

Daytime phone number____________________
Area code

Return entries with invoice in envelope provided. Each book in this shipment has two entry coupons—and the more coupons you enter, the better your chances of winning!

© 1989 HARLEQUIN ENTERPRISES LTD.

DINDL-3